# FOR THE LOVE OF...

M A COMLEY

JEAMEL PUBLISHING LIMITED

New York Times and USA Today bestselling author M A Comley
Published by Jeamel Publishing limited
Copyright © 2020 M A Comley
Digital Edition, License Notes

# ALSO BY M A COMLEY

Blind Justice (Novella)

Cruel Justice (Book #1)

Mortal Justice (Novella)

Impeding Justice (Book #2)

Final Justice (Book #3)

Foul Justice (Book #4)

Guaranteed Justice (Book #5)

Ultimate Justice (Book #6)

Virtual Justice (Book #7)

Hostile Justice (Book #8)

Tortured Justice (Book #9)

Rough Justice (Book #10)

Dubious Justice (Book #11)

Calculated Justice (Book #12)

Twisted Justice (Book #13)

Justice at Christmas (Short Story)

Justice at Christmas 2 (novella)

Prime Justice (Book #14)

Heroic Justice (Book #15)

Shameful Justice (Book #16)

Immoral Justice (Book #17)

Toxic Justice (Book #18)

Overdue Justice (Book #19)

Unfair Justice (a 10,000 word short story)

Irrational Justice (a 10,000 word short story)

Seeking Justice (a 15,000 word novella)

Caring For Justice (a 24,000 word novella)

Savage Justice (a 17,000 word novella Featuring THE UNICORN)

Vile Justice (A 17,000 word novella)

Clever Deception (co-written by Linda S Prather)

Tragic Deception (co-written by Linda S Prather)

Sinful Deception (co-written by Linda S Prather)

Forever Watching You (DI Miranda Carr thriller)

Wrong Place (DI Sally Parker thriller #1)

No Hiding Place (DI Sally Parker thriller #2)

Cold Case (DI Sally Parker thriller#3)

Deadly Encounter (DI Sally Parker thriller #4)

Lost Innocence (DI Sally Parker thriller #5)

Goodbye, My Precious Child (DI Sally Parker #6)

Web of Deceit (DI Sally Parker Novella with Tara Lyons)

The Missing Children (DI Kayli Bright #1)

Killer On The Run (DI Kayli Bright #2)

Hidden Agenda (DI Kayli Bright #3)

Murderous Betrayal (Kayli Bright #4)

Dying Breath (Kayli Bright #5)

Taken (Kayli Bright #6 coming March 2020)

The Hostage Takers (DI Kayli Bright Novella)

No Right to Kill (DI Sara Ramsey #1)

Killer Blow (DI Sara Ramsey #2)

The Dead Can't Speak (DI Sara Ramsey #3)

Deluded (DI Sara Ramsey #4)

The Murder Pact (DI Sara Ramsey #5)

Twisted Revenge (DI Sara Ramsey #6)

The Lies She Told (DI Sara Ramsey #7)

For The Love Of… (DI Sara Ramsey #8)

Run For Your Life (DI Sara Ramsey #9) Coming August 2020

I Know The Truth (A psychological thriller )

The Caller (co-written with Tara Lyons)

Evil In Disguise – a novel based on True events

Deadly Act (Hero series novella)

Torn Apart (Hero series #1)

End Result (Hero series #2)

In Plain Sight (Hero Series #3)

Double Jeopardy (Hero Series #4)

Criminal Actions (Hero Series #5)

Regrets Mean Nothing (Hero #6)

Sole Intention (Intention series #1)

Grave Intention (Intention series #2)

Devious Intention (Intention #3)

Merry Widow (A Lorne Simpkins short story)

It's A Dog's Life (A Lorne Simpkins short story)

A Time To Heal (A Sweet Romance)

A Time For Change (A Sweet Romance)

High Spirits

The Temptation series (Romantic Suspense/New Adult Novellas)

Past Temptation

Lost Temptation

Cozy Mystery Series

Murder at the Wedding

Murder at the Hotel

Murder by the Sea

Tempting Christa (A billionaire romantic suspense co-authored by Tracie Delaney #1)

Avenging Christa (A billionaire romantic suspense co-authored by Tracie Delaney #2)

# ACKNOWLEDGMENTS

Thank you as always to my rock, Jean, I'd be lost without you in my life.

Special thanks as always go to @studioenp for their superb cover design expertise.

My heartfelt thanks go to my wonderful editor Emmy Ellis, my proofreaders Joseph, Barbara and Jacqueline for spotting all the lingering nits.

Thank you also to Linda and Sandra from my amazing ARC group who allowed me to use their names in this book.

To Mary, gone, but never forgotten. I hope you found the peace you were searching for my dear friend.

*To JC - the fight goes on for justice. All my love, now and forever. xx*

## 1

"*I* remember that day, you were more than a little tipsy from what I can recall, and Daniel was far from happy when you entered the house and promptly passed out," Mandy stated, and they all laughed.

Her cheeks coloured up. Linda batted the comment away with her hand. "Bugger, don't remind me. That occasion is probably the sole reason I gave up drinking. I was mortified. Daniel and I had only been seeing one another for around two months, I think. He must have wondered what he was letting himself in for back then."

"Aww…he loved you from the very first date. He was like an eager puppy, always had his tongue hanging out. When are you going to do the right thing and set the date for the wedding? You've been engaged a few years now, haven't you?" Darla probed.

"I know. Work is hectic for both of us. It's aligning everything; we have our parents to consider, too. Mine are always jetting off somewhere enjoying their retirement while Daniel's parents live in Spain six months of the year."

"Sod them. Elope. Weddings can be a drain on resources nowadays. Mandy and I won't be offended if you dashed up to Gretna and came back to break the news, would we?"

"Gosh, no. It's your bloody day, and none of us should really matter. To some, a wedding is just an excuse for a good piss-up anyway."

Linda mulled over their suggestion, her pace slowing as they reached the taxi rank. "Okay, I'll have a word with Daniel tomorrow."

Mandy pointed at her. "And that's another thing…"

Linda rolled her eyes. She had an idea what her good friend was about to say. "Go on, surprise me."

"Why the heck are you two living separately after all these years together?"

"Don't ask. We both have properties. Neither one of us is willing to let our place go and move in with the other."

"What? Are you serious?" Mandy yelled, drawing attention from the crowd milling around them.

"What's so hard to believe? We're both super proud of the renovations we've carried out in our respective homes."

Darla shook her head in despair. "And that's what's held you back all these years?"

Linda shrugged. "I don't know, it might be a slight issue, who knows with these things?"

"Well, the easiest solution is for you both to sell up and buy a new house together. Do that, and your lives might just move on enough for you to decide on a date for the wedding. It's a no-brainer to me." Darla tutted and stepped forward to kiss Linda on the cheek. "Think about it. Take care. I'll be in touch at the weekend. Hectic period at work. I don't suppose I'll have much spare time in the evenings for the rest of the week."

"I suppose it's worth thinking about. I'll run it past Daniel, see what he thinks. Gotta go, girls. Thanks for a fabulous evening." She kissed Mandy and then opened the door to the taxi and slipped into the back seat. She gave the driver her address.

He replied with a surly grunt. He was an older man of Asian descent. She waved to her friends and took out her phone. Daniel always told her to text him once she was on her journey home. It was his way of knowing that she was safe after her night out with friends.

. . .

*O*N MY WAY HOME NOW. HAD A GREAT NIGHT BUT MISSED YOU LOTS. LOVE YOU. XX

He replied instantly. She imagined the phone being next to him as he watched the TV in the lounge. He wasn't really the type for going out with his friends, not during the week.

*G*LAD TO HEAR IT. WILL RING YOU TOMORROW. SLEEP WELL, MY BEAUTIFUL PRINCESS.

*S*he sent him three love hearts in return and sat there with a smile on her face for the rest of the journey. Once or twice she attempted to have a conversation with the driver, but each time it fell on deaf ears. Which left her wondering if he could speak any English at all.

*He must do, right? Otherwise, how would he be able to work in the UK?*

The dilemma swirled around her head for a few minutes—being a teacher, it was what she did. Sought out answers for different scenarios. Her head reeled; she had always been the type unable to switch off. Her lack of sleep was notorious. She loved her job and was totally committed to it. Maybe that was the stumbling block as to the real reason she and Daniel hadn't settled down properly together. She loved him, and there was no doubt he loved her, too. She was lucky in that respect. He was a romantic, always gave her flowers on the first day of the month, for no other reason than he was head over heels in love with her.

Linda smiled. She adored him. Loved to run her fingers through his blond hair, ruffling it playfully every time she passed by. He usually grinned up at her, loving the sentiment. Yes, the girls were right, it was about time she and Daniel got their act together and truly thought about their future. Maybe Darla's suggestion wasn't a crazy one after all. She'd run it past him over the next few days. It might be good to begin their married life in totally new surroundings where they wouldn't be that bothered about stepping on each other's toes.

She recognised her estate up ahead. The drive had been a swift one and filled with silence. In a way, she regarded the driver's reluctance to entertain her with his diatribe as a blessed relief. The taxi drew to a halt outside her house in the quiet street. There were a few lights still on in some of the downstairs rooms of her neighbours, but on the whole the street seemed as though most of its inhabitants had called it a day and gone to bed. Exactly where she'd be heading as soon as she'd fed her cat, Sailor, the second she stepped through the front door.

The driver pointed at the meter, still preferring not to speak to her. She withdrew a tenner from her purse, handed it to him and held her hand out for the change. If he thought he was getting a tip, he had another think coming. He dropped the coins in her hand, and she slipped out of the car. The taxi pulled away and, within seconds, a black van drew up beside her. Everything happened at warp speed after that. One moment she was standing at her gate, the next she had a hand slapped over her nose and mouth and was being bundled into the back of the vehicle. Her head was swimming; her eyelids drooped. Had they drugged her?

~

"*R*evenge, the sweetest morsel to the mouth that ever was cooked in Hell." He muttered the famous quote that was his driving force over and over while he drove the van out into the Herefordshire countryside, heading for the location he'd sourced the week before, during which time he'd hatched his audacious plan. This would be his first acquisition, but she definitely wouldn't be his last. Each of the women had failed him, but not only him. Tears misted his eyes, and he wiped them away.

The time had come to exact his revenge on all of them. The sleepless nights, the months—no, make that years—of torment deserved retribution. Throughout his life he'd been a peaceful person until that day...

That day, and the subsequent months, had taken a toll in more ways than one. Gone was his fun-loving nature, to be replaced by bitterness and the feeling of being cast aside and let down by those in charge. He'd done nothing wrong, except maybe partaking in a bit of weed in his formative years. That was all behind him now, and yet *she* persisted in telling all and sundry about the *one* bloody mistake which had blighted his past. He couldn't take any more, now he was at breaking point, and someone, if not all of them, had to pay for turning him into...well, whatever he'd become. They were about to find out, all of them. He wouldn't hold back either. He'd given his all to that relationship, for what? For her to tell him one day that it was all over and boot him out of the family home. The home he was paying for while she took up residence on the couch, day in, day out.

She had wanted for nothing. He had the paperwork to prove that. All the loans and debts he'd incurred, and they amounted to thousands, had been for her. To keep her happy. To stop her nagging. Winding him up and punishing him when he said she couldn't have the latest pair of boots that were on trend. But the clothes and shoes had soon escalated —she had wanted, no *demanded,* more from him. Now he was up to his ears in debt because she'd badgered him into taking out loans in his name for a car and a trailer to tow the horses he'd bought her, two of them to be precise. He'd furnished the whole house on interest-free loans, and she'd stolen all the furniture he was paying off. She'd left him the house along with the hefty mortgage and done a runner.

As if that all wasn't enough, things had escalated to far greater heights since then. She was twisted, sick in the head. She was the cause of all this, but to get to her, he had to finish off the others first. The ones who had refused to listen to him. The ones in power who were guilty of grossly letting him down. Her time would come, eventually, once the police were involved and the end was near. He'd take her down with him, if it came to that. He wasn't scared of meeting his maker, never had been. As far as he was concerned, his maker had constantly let him down over the years, from the day his father had dumped him, his sister and his mother at his grandparents' house and walked out of his life.

He'd needed counselling at the tender age of seven—a lot of good that had done him back then. If the counsellors had conducted their job properly, why was he now setting out on this vengeful journey?

He shook his head to clear his thoughts. He'd been driven to this, pure and simple. His life had imploded the day that bitch set out on her destructive path. She had him by the short and curlies while they had lived together, but that was nothing compared to what she'd done to him since they'd split. The lies she'd told about him were soul-destroying, and yet those in authority had believed her silver tongue and fake tears.

The bitch! She'd get hers, come the end.

Now, though, he had this one to deal with. Linda Strong. She was a decent enough person, he guessed, but she'd wronged him, robbed him of the one thing he had to cling on to in this life...and now she had to be punished for the sins she'd committed in his eyes, and what a humungous deal that was.

He parked outside the warehouse and opened the back of the van. He slid her limp body out and hoisted her over his shoulders, thankful she was a slender woman. He traipsed over the rubble-filled outer area and opened the warehouse door. It was derelict. Word had it that it was due to be knocked down soon. That news had forced his hand; he'd had to bring his plan forward a few weeks and now was relishing the idea of handing out his punishment.

These people had changed him dramatically over the years, intentionally or not. None of them had listened to his objections, his side of the story, only hers. She was such a twisted bitch. It had taken him years to realise she had a screw loose. She was the one in desperate need of a psychologist, not him. She was the one who set out to destroy him, and yet, she'd been allowed to get away with things. Not just once, no, repeatedly, the lies tripping off her tongue at a moment's notice.

That didn't let the other's off scot-free, though. They should have taken a step back, recognised who they were dealing with. The manipulative cow had always placed a smile on her face and accomplished so much more in life. The opposite had been true when she was with him. He'd needed to purchase everything she wished for in order to keep her happy. Her anger and bitterness had become inflexible and hard to handle, so he'd gone out of his way to ensure he kept the peace. He was a different character now, and the change in him could only be attributed to the time he'd spent with her.

He regretted cutting his family out of his life. Her wicked lies had caused him to do that without any consideration for how selfish she'd become.

Thankfully, his family had accepted his apology and were now all behind him in his quest to…

He shuddered and placed the woman on the ground with a thud. *What the hell will they think of me once they hear the news?*

He pushed the thought aside and concentrated on the task at hand. He'd rigged up a torture chamber for Miss Strong and secured her limp body in place on the contraption. He used the pulley to hoist the woman in place. She inched higher. He swivelled the plank of wood she was secured to over the large oil drum. Then he lowered her gently into its confines.

Linda coughed and spluttered into life. "No, please, don't do this. Help me!"

The magic words left her lips, and he pounced into action. He yanked on the heavy chain and winched her out of the murky, oil-skimmed water until she was level with him.

He grinned. "I hope you have a *strong* resilience? See what I did there?" He chuckled. But it didn't last. His expression turned serious once more.

"Please, why are you doing this to me? Who are you?"

He sniggered. "You don't recognise me." He ran his hand over his furry chin. "The beard did the trick, obviously. Enough of that, I'm here to punish you. For treating me so appallingly. Acting like you were some kind of goddess with a divine right to strip me of what's rightfully mine."

She frowned and closed her eyes. "I don't understand. What did you give me? My head…I can't think straight. I don't know what you're talking about."

"In other words, you're thick and you need me to spell it out for you. Go on, admit it."

"Okay, if that's what you want to believe, who am I to argue with you."

"Oh right, now you say that, and yet, over the last couple of years, that's all you've done, argue with me, even though I've been in the right and *she* was in the wrong. Why? Why believe her and not me?"

"Who? You're going to have to give me a hint. I haven't got a clue who you're talking about."

"Really? Come across many devious bitches in your line of work, do you? I'm guessing you do."

She blinked several times; he suspected it was to clear her vision. "I don't know who you're referring to, give me a name?"

"Ha…that would be too easy. If you survive what I have in store for you then you'll tell the police right away. I can't allow that to happen. I have a complex plan I need to follow and I won't accept any variance to my schedule."

"What schedule? What are you talking about?"

"You'll find out…oops, no you won't, because if I have my way, you're not going to be around long enough to find out."

"What are your intentions? Why have you targeted me when, as far as I know, I haven't done anything wrong?"

"You're delusional if you believe that. Maybe you're unaware of the power you have in your position, maybe not. I think it's the latter and you're bullshitting me. That's all I've had the past couple of years from people in your position, bullshit with a capital B. You don't try to help people, not men, anyway. Just because we have a dangly bit between our legs, it doesn't mean that we lack feelings. I'm compassionate and try to do the right thing in this world, however, people of your ilk refuse to comprehend that. Why is it you always come down on the woman's side? Why? You have no idea what that woman is guilty of. The things she's done over the years would turn your brown hair grey overnight, and yet, you all believed *her*. It was always her word against mine, and you all sided with her. Always! Shame on you."

"If I knew who you were talking about, maybe I'd be able to reconsider my thinking. Try to help you in some way."

"Bollocks. It's too late for that now. It's all too late. It's me who has been punished, who continues to be punished, all because you chose not to take my word for what was going on. Surely teachers are supposed to have some form of instinct, aren't they?"

"Yes, we work a lot on instinct. Oh God!"

"He's not going to help you. I take it you've recognised me now, am I right?"

"Yes. I have. Please, I did everything possible for you, but in the end, it was the governor's decision."

He tipped his head back and laughed. "And there we have it, you passing the buck. Own it! Go on, own the condemning decision you made, for once in your damn life."

"I won't, I can't. The decision wasn't mine to make, you have to believe me. I fought your corner so hard."

He took a few steps closer and backhanded her with such force her head snapped to the side. "Don't bullshit me, you're guilty of listening to her lies. You're guilty of failing me. But most importantly you're guilty of failing *him*. And for that you need to be punished. Revenge will be mine when all this is over and done with. Something to cling on to and ease the pain all of you have caused. People in power need to be held accountable for their erroneous actions. You will be the first. But I'll leave you with this nugget: you can be sure that the others will receive the same punishment as you. Some more violent than others, nevertheless, you will all lose your lives. The aim being that you never put another person through the heartbreak I have suffered over the past couple of years."

Linda sobbed and cried out, "Please, please reconsider what you're about to do. I'd like to help you. We can turn the decision around. At least let me try for you."

"Where were you when I needed you two years ago? You could have said all this back then. Instead, you choose to do it now, selfishly, when your own life hangs in the balance, literally. No, the world is going to be a better place without you meddling in folks' lives. Good-bye, Miss Strong!"

He lowered her into the barrel and peered over the rim. She struggled, thrashed her hands around in the water until her movements stopped and the bubbles ceased to break the surface.

She was gone. On to the next one.

## 2
_____

"*O*h, joy of joys, here we go again!" Sara used the siren to get through the congested traffic blocking their path.

"Do you ever feel like you're on a hamster wheel?" Carla complained from the passenger seat beside her.

"All the bloody time. Still, I have the weekend to look forward to."

"Lucky you. What I wouldn't give for a weekend away in Scotland right now. I'm knackered. All these wedding plans are so bloody draining. Men have it easy, don't they? It's the women who do most of the work in that department, right?"

"Actually, not in our case. Mark is throwing in his tuppence worth, which I truly appreciate. You'll get there. Can't you have a word with Gary if he's not pulling his weight?"

"I don't want it to come across as if I'm nagging him. His recovery from the accident pretty much takes up most of his time. He's getting there. He's now doing a few shifts more each week, almost up to twenty-five hours now. Doing that takes a toll on him, and he tends to fall asleep in the chair in the evening."

"It must be hard on both of you."

"It is. Not that I'm one to whinge, not really. I'm grateful for having him in my life after the way Andrew treated me. Cheating bastard."

"Do you ever see him?"

"Nope. I dread to think how I'd react if I ever laid eyes on him, especially if he had another woman on his arm."

"It doesn't do to be bitter, love. Jeez…I've learned that over the years to my cost. My state of mind before Mark came into my life… well, it's hard to put a finger on how to describe it really. You witnessed it first-hand, what would you say?"

Carla's eyes widened, and her hands flew up. "Whoa, now wait just a minute. I ain't going down that route. There's a time for honesty about things, just not in this case. I need this job. If I start criticising you, where the fuck does that leave me? In a sodding igloo out in the Arctic, is my guess."

Sara chortled. "You're an idiot, as if I'd hold anything against you."

"There's that old adage of elephants never forgetting."

Sara shook her head and laughed. "Idiot. We're partners, damn good ones, too, I might add."

"Yeah and I'd prefer to keep it that way, if it's all the same to you."

"Okay, I hear you. How far now?" Sara glanced at the satnav. "Eight minutes out. I wonder what we're going to find."

"Umm…a corpse in a lay-by."

"Add having a smart mouth to your list of attributes." She faced Carla for a split second and spotted her grin. She took one hand off the steering wheel and playfully punched Carla in the thigh.

They chatted generally about the wedding arrangements they both had in place until Sara arrived at the scene.

"This is a bit out in the sticks, isn't it?"

"Yep, good place for an offender to dump a body, though, I'm guessing."

They exited the car and walked towards the SOCO van already at the scene. "It's about time you two showed up. Talk about being late for the damn party," Lorraine Dixon, the resident pathologist, grumbled.

Sara tutted. "Wind your neck in, we got here as soon as we could."

Lorraine continued to prepare herself for the scene. She gathered her shocking red hair and tied it up in a tight ponytail. "You'd better get suited and booted."

"Got some supplies for us?"

"Christ, you're always the same, always out for what you can get out of me."

Sara laughed. "Are you for real? Who's rattled your cage this morning?"

"No one. Don't start on me, Ramsey, just leave it."

Sara and Carla exchanged concerned glances. Lorraine was usually a happy-go-lucky type of person. Someone had clearly rubbed her up the wrong way.

"Do you need to take five minutes out for a chat?"

"If I didn't have a crime scene on my hands, I might take you up on that. As things stand, I'd rather get on with it, if it's all the same to you. I apologise for my unprofessionalism. Let's start again, shall we?"

"Fine by me. I'm always available if you need to vent about anything, you know that."

Lorraine reached into the back of the van and removed two extra paper suits which she passed on to Sara and Carla. "I know. Just ignore me. I shouldn't allow my personal problems to interfere with work."

"Hey, don't be so hard on yourself, you're human, just like the rest of us. You're usually so effervescent, I suppose it stands out like a sore thumb when your mood is different."

"Yeah, that's me, folks, the clown at the party. Well, not any more."

Sara placed a hand on her forearm. "This can wait, the corpse isn't going anywhere. We need to get things worked out with you before it hampers your work."

Lorraine's eyebrows shot into her hairline. "It's not likely to, but thanks for the vote of confidence."

"Shit! Me and my big mouth. I didn't mean to make things worse."

"You haven't. The truth is, I'm not ready to discuss what's troubling me yet. Let's get on. My priority is getting this body back to base."

Sara and Carla slipped into their protective gear and followed Lorraine to the scene. SOCO technicians were doing their bit, analysing the ground around the body and taking the relative photos of the crime scene.

"Was she killed here?" Sara asked. She had a rough idea what Lorraine's answer was going to be before she said it.

"Nope. She was moved here after the poor woman's soul departed this earth."

"I figured as much. She seems wet, or is that because we had a brief downpour earlier this morning?"

"It's hard to judge. I'll need to cut her open to find out the cause of death. As this isn't the projected crime scene, I've instructed the team to work swiftly and get the corpse back to the lab. It's my intention to begin the post-mortem ASAP."

"Thanks, that sounds great. Any marks on her? Any form of ID?"

Lorraine angled her chin and pointed it at a handbag which had been placed in an evidence bag. "Full ID in there I shouldn't wonder."

"Interesting. In most cases, the killer does everything they can to hide the victim's identity."

"Yep, that was my first thought, too. I had a quick peep. She's Linda Strong, a teacher at Lossworth Primary School."

Carla jotted down the details in her notebook. "And what could a primary school teacher have done to have hacked someone off enough to kill her?"

"Given a bad school report to someone's little darling perhaps," Lorraine quipped, her recent anger giving way to her usual sense of warped humour.

"Hmm...not one I've come across in the past during my time on the force, either around here or up in Liverpool." Sara shuddered. "Stereotypical point of view coming up, aren't they supposed to be classed as whiter-than-white type of people?"

Carla sniggered. "Maybe in Jean Brodie's day."

"I think Carla's right. Where have you been, Inspector? These days anything goes, doesn't it? I'm not getting involved in the whys and wherefores of why someone set out to kill this woman, I'd rather deal with the facts. She's dead, and someone did this to her. Whether her career choice had something to do with her murder is neither here nor there for me."

"All right, it was a mere observation on my part, no need to come down heavy on me," Sara sniped back.

"Okay, as I said, let's deal in facts. From what I can tell, the woman's lower half clothing is intact, which would signify that she hasn't been sexually assaulted. That's a plus, if only for her family's sake."

"Right, a blessing for them, not for her, though. I need more to go on, Lorraine."

"And you'll get it, once I've performed my magic back at base."

Sara tilted her head. "In other words, you're telling us to get out of your hair, right?"

"No, not telling you, I'm asking you politely. You can see the situation. She's got no marks on her, except a slight redness to her cheek. She could have bumped into something..."

"Like someone's hand perhaps," Sara chipped in.

"Possibly. Again, that's all assumption at this point. Any more questions?"

"No, we'll just take a butcher's through her ID, see what we can gather from that and leave you to it."

"Thanks."

Lorraine bent down beside the corpse, and Sara and Carla moved over to the evidence bag with the victim's handbag inside.

A SOCO technician removed the bag and handed it to Sara. She extracted the woman's purse, confirmed her identity on the credit cards and searched further for an address. It came in the form of a letter from the school, which was where she presumed Lorraine had obtained her information regarding the woman's career.

Carla jotted down the victim's address and that of the school, and Sara tucked the letter back in the handbag. She dug around for more clues and stumbled across a photo of the victim with either a few friends or family members.

Sara turned the picture over. There was nothing written on the back to confirm who the other people were. "That's a shame. Okay, we've got a start. Let's try her home address first."

"Want me to contact the station, see what Christine can find out about the victim?"

"Good idea. Let's set the ball rolling on that one ASAP."

They made their way back to the car, removed their protective gear and deposited it in the black bag pinned down by a rock next to the SOCO van. Then they jumped back in the car.

Carla placed the call to the station, and Sara set up the satnav with the victim's address. Within fifteen minutes they were pulling up outside a large semi-detached house in the nicer part of town. Sara left Carla in the car and rang the doorbell. She waited a few seconds and then tried it again. No answer. She shook her head at Carla who shrugged. Sara took a punt that one of the neighbours might be able to fill in the blanks for them.

She knocked on the adjoining neighbour's house. There was no response. She made her way back up the path and tried the neighbour on the other side.

An old lady opened the door. She had a yapping dog in her arms. "Hello, don't mind Tiddles, she'll calm down in a moment. Hush now, let me listen, will you, blasted dog."

Sara produced her warrant card. "Hello, I'm sorry to disturb you. I'm DI Sara Ramsey. I wondered if you could tell me a little bit about one of your neighbours."

"Depends which one. Just because I'm retired and at home all day, it doesn't mean I know everything that goes on around here, you know."

"I didn't mean to suggest you would. The lady concerned is Linda Strong, do you know her?"

"Ah yes, I can definitely help you there. Want to do this inside?"

"Why not? Thanks." Sara followed the woman, who walked with a slight stoop up the narrow corridor and into a kitchen that was dated from a bygone era. "Take a seat. Want a cuppa, dear? I was about to make myself one anyway."

"You're very kind, only if you have coffee."

"I don't, I'm sorry. It's tea or nothing."

"I'm fine then, don't let me stop you having one."

"I won't." The woman placed the dog on the floor. It scampered out of the room. "Gone to her bed in the lounge, by the fire no doubt. Only gets out for three things that one: to go to the toilet, to eat and to follow me to the door when the damn bell rings. What did you want to know about Linda? Not in any trouble, is she?"

Sara cringed. She had no intention of telling the woman the nature of her visit, not without telling the next of kin first. "No, it's nothing like that. I'm carrying out a general enquiry. Does she share her home with anyone?"

"Yes, Daniel. Don't ask me what his last name is. Lovely man, he is, often drops in on me for a cuppa and asks if I need any help around the house, that sort of thing."

"That's nice of him. Have they lived here long?"

"It was Linda's house before he came along. They're engaged, getting married next year, I think. It's still in the planning stages, last I heard. Like I say, nice chap, would do anything for you. They both are, often drop off at the supermarket to do some shopping for me if my arthritis plays up now and again. They're lovely neighbours, I couldn't ask for better ones. Wait a minute, silly me, he doesn't live there, he has his own house, I believe, although he's a frequent visitor."

"That's great to hear. Especially nowadays. Not many people tend to sing their neighbour's praises, I can assure you." Her heart went out to the victim and her family with a wedding to look forward to. All that would go to pot now that Linda had been murdered, of course.

She wagged a finger. "I can believe it. It's dreadful how some folks treat their fellow human beings. I sometimes switch off the news during the evening when it all gets too much for me. The violence is just horrendous. Your lot have got a hard job on your hands these days. My brother used to be a copper, you know, when there were coppers walking the beat."

"A distant memory to have coppers out there," Sara agreed.

"Ah, the good old days. He often detected crimes when they were still just a figment of the youths' imagination. He always told me he could spot a kiddie about to get into mischief from a mile away. I dare say, the kids on the street today would sooner stick a knife in someone than have a discussion."

"I think you're right. The world has become an impossible place to live in at times. You feel safe living around here, though, don't you?"

"I do. I'm lucky to live here. This is definitely the better part of town. We rarely have any trouble in this street, I can tell you."

"Good to know. Getting back to Linda and Daniel… Do you happen to know where Daniel works?"

"I do that. See that over there?" She pointed at a model aircraft of what Sara thought could be a bomber from the Second World War, sitting on the kitchen dresser.

"May I?" She stepped closer to take a better look.

"Aye, go ahead. Daniel owns a hobby shop in town. I told him my father flew one of those in the war during the D-Day landings to support the troops, and the next week he produced that. Bloody broke down in tears, I did. What an incredible gesture. No one has ever done something as kind as that for me, I can tell you."

Sara returned to her seat at the round kitchen table, her throat clogged up with tears. "How wonderful. I don't suppose you happen to know the name of the shop?"

The woman chewed her lip and shook her head. "No, I can't say I do, dear. Sorry, I don't suppose there are too many shops like that in town, do you?"

"I'll find it, I'm sure. Okay, I'd better get going now. Thanks for taking time out of your day to speak with me."

The woman rose from her chair on tottery legs.

"Stay there, finish your drink. I can find my own way out."

"If you're sure. Once I'm sat down, my bloody hips seize up."

"I'm sorry to hear that. Want me to help you back into the lounge? It'll be too cold out here for you, I suspect."

"You're very kind. That would be fabulous. I should use my walking stick. I always forget the darn thing. Still in there sitting by my chair, I shouldn't wonder."

Sara smiled and eased the woman out of her chair. They wandered back through the hallway and into the lounge. Tiddles was indeed curled up snoring gently in her basket by the gas fire that was on a low heat.

"Where do you want to sit?"

"There, that's my chair, dear. Thank you."

"You're welcome. I'll be off now. Take care of yourself."

"I will. It was nice to meet you."

Sara peered at the black clouds overhead and made a dash for the car. "Phew, that was close." The rain splattered the windscreen in large spots.

"Yep. I have news."

"Go on." Sara turned in her seat to face Carla.

"Linda Strong was flagged up on the system as a missing person."

"Okay. So, when was she reported missing, and by who?"

"The boyfriend, or should I say, her fiancé. On Wednesday of this week."

"Not long ago then. I thought you were going to tell me that she'd been held for months and then killed."

"Nope. Lorraine didn't give us any indication of the time of death, did she?"

"No. She wasn't in the best of moods, so I didn't want to probe too much. She'll get back to us soon with the PM results, no doubt. Right, I have news as well. The neighbour I just spoke to told me that the fiancé runs a hobby shop in Hereford. That shouldn't be hard to track down, should it? You do that while I head back into the centre." Sara started the engine and set off.

"Here we go. According to Google Maps, it's close to Primark. Difficult to park around there."

Sara grinned. "That's never stopped me before."

# 3

___

The shop was quiet, two men standing behind the counter fiddling with bits from a model train, but no customers in sight.

Sara produced her ID and smiled at them. "Hi, I'm looking for Daniel Pope."

The older man frowned and nodded. "That would be me. Is this about Linda? Have you found her?"

"Is there somewhere private we can have a chat, sir?"

"Through the back. Stu, mind the fort."

"Sure. Good luck," the younger man replied. He picked up the instructions for the model they'd been building together and studied them.

Daniel showed Sara and Carla through to a cluttered storeroom at the rear of the shop. The rain pummelled a Velux window over the lean-to attached to the small room.

"Sorry, I'd offer you a seat but I don't have any. We tend to have our lunch break et cetera out there, in the shop. Anyway, you don't want to hear all that. What news have you got for me?"

*Strictly speaking, he wasn't the next of kin but they are engaged so they're as near as dammit.* "Daniel, it's with regret I have to tell you that Linda's body was found this morning out at Monkhide."

"Her body. Are you telling me…she's dead?"

"Yes, although a next of kin will be required to formally identify her."

He ran a shaking hand through his hair and turned around to face the courtyard outside the back door of the small kitchenette. "Oh shit! This can't be true. It can't be her. I don't believe it. Not Linda, she can't be…dead. Why? How?"

"I'm sorry. We've yet to determine all the details. With your help we'd like to piece her final hours together, if that's all right with you?"

He faced them with tears brimming his piercing blue eyes. "This is unbelievable. Of course I'll do what I can to help you, but at the same time you need to appreciate how shocking this is for me."

"We do. I promise. Do you want to make yourself a drink?"

"No. Go on, what do you need to know?"

"Okay. When was the last time you saw Linda?"

"Wednesday lunchtime. She met me for a bite to eat because she was going out with a couple of friends for a meal and the to the cinema in the evening."

Sara saw out of the corner of her eye that Carla was taking notes. "Where did you go for lunch?"

"We grabbed a sandwich in the town centre at the café in the square there."

"Did she seem troubled or anxious about anything?"

"No. Nothing. She was her usual cheerful self. Wait…my head is clearing a bit now. When you say her body was found, are you telling me she had an accident of sorts? I noticed her car was outside the house when I called round there yesterday."

"Umm…no, we're waiting for confirmation from the pathologist but we have reason to believe Linda was murdered."

"What? I…just…don't understand that. How?" He staggered back a few steps as if Sara had landed a sucker punch to his gut.

"We don't have anything else we can tell you as yet. I'm sorry."

"Oh God. She was such a good person. Why on earth would someone take her life like that?"

"Again, we're doing our best to try and work that out. When you said goodbye on Wednesday, did she tell you she'd be in touch later that evening?"

"Yes, as she went out on a 'school night' if you will, she was intending to be home earlyish. I told her to ring me when she got home. She texted me instead. We live separately, for now, until the... wedding next year. Oh shit! What about her parents? They'll be devastated. Have you told them yet?"

"No, this is our first stop. We'll visit them next, if that's what you want."

"I couldn't face telling them. News like this could kill either one of them. They're both in ill health, you see. Mr Strong has a dodgy ticker, and Cilla is going through chemo for breast cancer."

Sara shook her head. "We'll take that on board when we tell them. Thank you for the warning. Getting back to Linda... So, as far as you were concerned, she'd arrived home safely. Is that right?"

"Wait, I've got her text here." He fished his mobile out of the back pocket of his jeans and showed it to Sara. "On her way, she said."

"Thanks. Okay, have you noticed any changes in her in the past few months?"

"No. Apart from her getting very excited about the wedding we were planning."

"Which was due to take place when?"

"June next year. We've booked the reception, paid up front for that, the flowers, the dresses and my suit...and now...she's gone!" He placed his hand against his cheek.

"I'm so sorry. My heart goes out to you at this sad time. Are you sure you can't think of anything that may have upset her recently?"

"No, she wasn't the type to get upset. She was the most placid person you're ever likely to meet. Her pupils adore her. She was given far more presents than the rest of the teachers put together. They wouldn't do that if they despised her, would they? Shit! It's just dawning on me now, the implications, I mean. We were planning to start a family of our own after we settled down, and now that's not going to happen, and I...shit! How am I going to cope without her in my life?"

"It'll be hard. Do you have good friends and close family living nearby?"

"Yes, we're both from Hereford. But it won't be the same as having Linda here with me. She was my life."

A lump formed in Sara's throat, and she did her best to swallow it down without making it too obvious. "What about former boyfriends? Did Linda ever have any problems there?"

"No, she was still in touch with two of them. Neither of them would be responsible for killing her. They're both happily married."

"Can you give us their names?"

"Michael and Jeremy, but I couldn't tell you their surnames, sorry."

"That's fine. Maybe her parents will be able to tell us."

"Possibly. Go easy on them, won't you?"

"You have my word. Is there anything else you can possibly tell us?"

"Like what? My head's a mess, I can't think straight."

"What about at school? You mentioned she was very popular with the pupils. Do you think that could have led to jealousy from any of her colleagues?"

"No. I can't see that at all. Maybe you'll need to speak to her boss, sorry, the headmistress about that. Linda didn't really discuss the ins and outs of her job. The same as I don't tend to. Pretty mundane, both of our jobs really."

"Teaching? Is that what she felt?"

"No, that was my perception. By mundane, I meant that she did the same thing day in, day out, no variance to it, similar to here, I suppose. Am I making any sense? Because it doesn't sound like it to me. I never waffle. Is that what death does to you? Makes your head hurt?"

"Grief and the shock of hearing such dreadful news is bound to take its toll on you, either now or in the future. It's important for you to seek help or advice if you need it."

"I will, but it won't bring Linda back, will it?"

"Sadly not. I can arrange for counselling for you, if you think it will help."

"I don't think it will. I'm not a man to openly discuss what is going on in my head, but thanks anyway."

"The offer still stands. Here's one of my cards. If you think of anything else, will you promise to ring me?"

"Yep, I'll do that. When can I see her?"

"If you give us your phone number, we'll pass it on to the pathologist, Lorraine, and she will be in touch soon to make the arrangements."

"Thanks. Do you need anything else from me?"

"That's all for now. If anything comes to light, I might need to check back with you, if that's okay? Oh wait, yes, perhaps you can give me the names and details of the friends you said Linda was out with on Wednesday?"

"Hang on, I'll need to get my phone." He scrolled through and handed the phone to Carla to jot down two numbers. "Darla and Mandy, they were very close. Maybe Linda confided in one of them about any concerns she may have had in recent weeks."

"We'll get in touch with them. Thanks for the information. We'll leave you with our condolences and our assurance that we will do our best to find her killer."

"Thanks, that means a lot."

The three of them re-entered the shop. He opened the door for them and bid them farewell.

Outside, Sara cursed. "Bloody traffic warden on the rampage. Haven't they got anything better to bloody do?"

Carla chased after her and shouted, "I did warn you."

"You can leave the bloody 'I told yous' alone." Sara stormed up to the traffic warden and flashed her warrant card under the officious middle-aged man's nose. "I'm a copper, on police business."

"And how am I supposed to know that? There's nothing official left on the dashboard. Anyway, it's too late now, your ticket has been written."

"What the actual—"

He held his hand up to prevent her saying another word. "If any profanity leaves your mouth, I'm warning you, I will report you to your superiors."

Sara swallowed down the tirade of abuse she'd summoned up and was about to let loose on the bureaucratic twerp. "My lips are sealed. It's my mistake. I apologise. Is there any way you can cancel the ticket?"

"Nope, not once I've written it. It's more than my job's worth." Then, for good measure, he slapped the yellow-and-white sticker on her windshield.

Sara tore it off, pressed the key fob and got in the car. Then she let rip.

Carla burst out laughing beside her.

"Not the response I was hoping for. I take it your sympathy gene didn't report for duty this morning, partner."

"Sorry. You're bloody hilarious when you let rip."

Sara switched on the engine. "I'm glad I amuse you. Right, let's get over to break the news to her parents. Oh, the joys of being a blasted copper."

"You love it!"

"Fortunately, I do. Sometimes," she added mischievously.

# 4

*L*inda's parents lived out at Hope-under-Dinmore.

Sara pulled into the Queenswood café en route. "Sorry, I know we should get there, but I'm in dire need of sustenance. A coffee and cake to set us up for the day, what do you say?"

"I say you're nuts and have your priorities all wrong, but if you're paying, then who am I to object?"

"Exactly. What do you fancy? I love this place. Mark and I come up here quite a bit now, since you brought me here the first time. Gosh, that seems such a long time ago, doesn't it?"

"It must be a couple of years. Not long after you moved here, wasn't it?"

"Yep, I think you're right. Way back when I was full of grief, wondering which way my life was heading, and now look at me, planning my wedding to an absolutely adorable guy."

"Yeah, you've certainly come a long way in a short space of time, I'll grant you that one."

They left the car and joined the small queue inside the café. Carla made her way to a table in the far corner. The queue decreased, giving Sara the chance to see what delicious cakes they had on offer. She plumped for a slice of coffee-and-walnut cake for each of them, accompanied by two Americanos.

After paying and throwing a tip in the cup on the counter, Sara carried the tray to the table and unloaded it. "I know, the slices are huge. Bang goes the diet for the day."

"Day? You mean the week. Thanks for this. My turn next time."

"Deal. I know I'm delaying the inevitable by stopping off here. You know how much I detest breaking bad news."

"I know, I don't think any copper enjoys that side of the job. Quite surprised you're keen to do it on a full stomach, though."

"The pull of this place was too much. On the drive up here, all I could think about was stuffing my face, not planning out what I should say to grieving relatives. My bad."

"Extremely bad. This cake is scrummy, though, so I'm willing to forgive you. What about the friends? Are we going to visit them as well today?"

"I'd like to, depends how the day pans out. We might be a while with the parents, another reason to get something to eat early."

They tucked into their cake and left the murder case alone for the time being.

"I know we touched on the subject briefly earlier, but you didn't really say much, how are the plans for the wedding coming along?" Carla asked.

Sara finished her mouthful and smiled. "Good, good. Really good, actually. What about you?"

"I think you're way ahead of us. Gary's recovery is taking longer than anticipated which is making him antsy. If I dare to raise the subject, he snaps my head off."

Sara placed her fork on the plate and pushed it away. "What? Is there a rift between you now?"

"I don't know what to call it, if I'm honest. Rift might be a little extreme."

Sara touched the back of Carla's hand. "I'm sorry, love. I hope you get it sorted soon."

"We will. Hey, I don't want to rain on your parade, boss, feel free to let me know how your plans are progressing."

"Maybe another time. Only if you're sure. Don't be afraid to tell me to shut the hell up, though, if it all gets a bit too much for you."

"I won't. That was lovely. I'm stuffed now. Shall we go?"

They both downed the rest of their coffees and left the café, waving to the friendly assistants behind the counter as they passed.

Sara checked her teeth the second she got in the car and removed a few cake crumbs which had settled in between the larger gaps. "Right, here we go. Their house is five minutes up the road, enough time for us to get our shit together and put on a sad façade."

"I don't think that'll be difficult once we lay eyes on the parents and their grief begins to show."

"True enough."

The Strongs' home was a detached cottage situated halfway down a country lane. Mrs Strong opened the door. She seemed a little frail, and her voice faltered a touch when she asked who they were.

"Hello, Mrs Strong, we're DI Sara Ramsey and DS Carla Jameson. Would it be all right if we came inside for a moment or two?"

"Yes, come in out of this damn rain." Once they were standing in the hallway, she asked, "May I ask what this visit is about?"

"Maybe we can take a seat somewhere first. Is your husband around?"

"Sounds serious. I'll give him a call; he's tinkering in his man shed. Why don't you go in the lounge and make yourselves comfortable in there?"

"Thank you."

She used a walking stick to travel the length of the narrow passage. Sara entered the lounge and sat on the sofa with Carla. They waited a full five minutes until the couple graced them with their presence.

"Sorry to keep you waiting. I had a cake in the oven I needed to keep an eye on, and Patrick wanted to wash his hands."

"Hello, ladies, what's this all about then? Don't be shy," Patrick Strong said, his tone filled with frivolity and humour.

Sara cleared her throat and motioned for the couple to take a seat.

Once they were both seated, Mr Strong put one of his arms around his wife's shoulders and the other hand on her knee.

"We've just come from having a word with Daniel," Sara said.

The couple glanced at each other, their frowns matching, and then looked back at Sara.

"Go on," Patrick urged.

*Shit! They don't know she's missing.*

"I'm not sure how much you know about your daughter's disappearance..."

Patrick raised one of his hands. "Wait, did I just hear right? Our daughter's disappearance?"

"You did. I take it you're not aware of the situation then?"

"You've got that right. How long has she been missing?"

"Since Wednesday evening. I have to ask, why wouldn't her fiancé have told you?"

The couple both shook their heads. Mrs Strong sobbed, and Mr Strong appeared to be getting angrier by the minute, judging by the intense colour filling his cheeks.

"That's what I'd like to know."

"Now, in Daniel's defence, he did warn us that you were both in poor health. Maybe he didn't want to cause you any unnecessary stress."

"Possibly," Mr Strong relented. "So, are you going to tell us what this visit is all about?"

"It is with regret that we have to tell you that your daughter's body was found this morning. It looks like she has been murdered."

"What? How? Who?" Mr Strong stuttered out the words at the same time his wife's head collapsed against his chest and her sobbing increased. She let out a desperate scream at one point as the information sank in.

Sara found the scene traumatic because of her own loss in life. It took her back to how she'd been forced to overcome Philip's death. She shook her head to shake the image free. This was neither the time nor the place to dwell on her own misfortunes in life.

"I'm very sorry. There was no easy way of telling you."

The couple held each other tightly, lost for words for the next five minutes or so. The time dragged, but Sara understood their need to process the information. Grief affected people in different ways. In her experience, they either became angry or inconsolable.

Finally, Mr Strong reached for the box of tissues off the coffee table and placed it in his wife's lap. He withdrew one for himself and blew his nose on it. "I'm sorry. No, I'm not, we have a right to grieve for our beautiful daughter. Why would anyone kill her? Was it a one-off attack? Or was she intentionally targeted by someone evil?"

Sara sighed. "We're at the start of our investigation. Our first task is to inform the next of kin and try to find out as much detail about the victim as we can. Maybe, if you're up to it, you wouldn't mind giving us a little background on your daughter. I know it's asking a lot of you at this sad time. I quite understand if the request comes across as insensitive."

"It does, but we want to help. If there's a killer out there, they need to be caught. What I'm struggling to understand is why they chose Linda. She's always got on well with people. I know this will probably come across as a biased statement, but she didn't have a bad bone in her. She ran for charities. When I say ran, I mean several marathons a year. She trained hard every week, gave up on so much to give to others. It doesn't make sense why someone would kill her." Mr Strong tutted and shook his head.

"Perhaps you can tell us if she's fallen out with anyone in the past? A former partner maybe? Someone likely to have a vendetta with her?"

"No, no one. What did Daniel say? I can't believe he left us in the dark about this."

"He told us Linda had a couple of boyfriends in her past but that she was still friends with them."

"There you go then. That's what I would say as well. She's such a caring woman. She's a teacher at a primary school, you know."

"We know. That's going to be our next stop. Are you sure you can't think of anything that might have formed a cloud over your daughter's character?"

"Definitely not!" Mr Strong snapped. "Why can't this be a stranger who did this? Why are you here asking us these questions, interrogating us, when you should be out there searching for this vile individual? How did she die?"

"As I said, we need to do the groundwork first. It's important for us to find out what Linda was like and the people she mixed with. Today should give us those answers, and then tomorrow we'll be doing the heavy lifting on the case. In the meantime, I have my team back at the station working their socks off. The pathologist is also doing her bit and ascertain the cause of death for us by the end of the day, I presume."

"Good to know. In a nutshell, our daughter is a peace-loving person, and yes, I'm aware I used the present tense. My reason behind that is..." His resolve caved in.

It was Mrs Strong's turn to comfort him.

"Would you like me to make you a drink?" Sara asked.

"That would be kind, thank you," Mrs Strong responded.

Sara went to stand, but Carla placed a hand on her arm. "I'll do it."

"Thanks." Sara appreciated Carla's thoughtfulness; however, she had been eager to leave the room to get some fresh air what with her own emotions in turmoil.

Carla returned a few minutes later, holding a tray with four cups and saucers and a pot of tea.

"Not for me, thanks, partner."

Carla shrugged, as if to apologise for not being able to track down any coffee.

The couple had remained quiet in Carla's absence. She handed the Strongs' their drinks and took her seat again next to Sara on the couch.

"I've thought about what you asked and I can't for the life of me think of a time when Linda fell out with anyone. If she was a bitter person, why would she remain in touch with her ex-boyfriends? It doesn't make sense. Unless I'm missing something," Mr Strong said, his head shaking in disbelief. "I'm confused and bewildered by the loss of our beautiful daughter, if you must know."

"Knowing that she had no known enemies will help to steer the investigation. It will force us to concentrate on issues other than her character. So thank you for that. Are you both going to be all right? Do you have any other children, or someone I can call to come and sit with you?"

"No, we'll survive. Cilla and I are stronger than people believe us to be. Our health might be waning, but there is nothing wrong with our minds. That's right, isn't it, love?" Mr Strong pecked his wife on the cheek.

She smiled weakly at him in return and nodded. "Yes. But, Patrick, she's gone. I will never hear her on the phone or hold her in my arms again. How will I survive, knowing that?"

He patted his wife's hand. "We're going to have to, love. We'll get through this. It might be the highest mountain we've ever had to climb during our lives, but we'll conquer and do it together."

An emotional lump embedded itself in Sara's throat, and she gave a slight cough to clear it. "My heart goes out to you both. I promise we won't stop until we find the person who did this to Linda."

"Thank you," Mr Strong said. His head dipped to his chest, and his shoulders shook.

His wife hugged him and ran a soothing hand over his back. "There, there, we'll get through this together, Patrick. You and me against the world, just like when we were first married."

The couple were clearly devoted to each other, and Sara regretted coming here and wrecking their lives with a few inane words of sympathy.

Carla finished her cup of tea and placed it back on the tray.

Sara took that as their cue to leave. "Well, we'd better go now. If you're sure we can't do anything else for you before we leave."

"No. We'd rather you go and find the bastard who has torn our lives apart." Mr Strong straightened his shoulders and used the arm of the couch to ease himself out of the chair. He got to the hallway and then stopped and fell backwards.

"Patrick, are you all right?" his wife shouted.

Sara shot out of her seat and crouched beside the old man. "Sir, you need to tell me what's going on. Where does it hurt? Carla, ring for an ambulance."

Mr Strong placed a hand over his chest. "It's my heart." His voice was weak and etched in pain.

Sara feared for this man's life. Any colour he'd had in his cheeks previously had now faded. She glanced over her shoulder at Carla and widened her eyes.

Carla stared back at her as she urgently spoke into her phone. "Yes, it's an emergency. Suspected heart attack."

"Come on, Patrick, let's make you more comfortable on the couch." She helped the old man to swing his legs up onto the couch and propped his head up with a couple of cushions. "There, how are you feeling now?"

"Worse. A lot worse. I don't think I'm long for this world."

"Please, Patrick, don't think like that. Try to remain positive. Help is on the way, it'll be here soon, I promise." She turned to Carla, more out of hope than expectation.

Carla raised three fingers. "Thanks, yes, I'll stay on the line. Please, tell them to hurry."

"They're on their way, Patrick. Stay with us. Can I get you anything? Do you have medication you should be taking?"

"Oh my, yes, he should. There, over on the cabinet. Pop one under his tongue, it might, no, it should help," Mrs Strong said. Her hand shook as she pointed at the piece of furniture.

Sara shot across the room, retrieved the bottle, tipped a tablet into her hand and returned to help Mr Strong sit up. He was gone. His lips blue. "No. Don't you dare die on me. I won't allow this to happen." She removed the cushions, placing Patrick flat on his back and began CPR.

Mrs Strong broke down and screamed, adding to Sara's stress levels, which were tipping maximum by now.

Sirens wailed in the distance. Sara kept up the CPR while Carla raced to the door to let the paramedics in. Sara pumped until two men in uniform entered the room. She stepped aside, and one of the paramedics took over the CPR while the other one placed his bag on the floor and unzipped it. He withdrew the defibrillator and placed the pads on Patrick's bare chest. The poor man's body leapt off the couch a few inches, numerous times, as the paramedics did their best to revive him. But it was too late. He was gone. The two paramedics agreed to call time on their efforts.

Sara eased herself into the seat next to Mrs Strong and threw a comforting arm around her shoulder. "I'm so very sorry for your loss. We did everything we could to try to save him."

She didn't answer. She sobbed and sobbed, tears flowing freely down her pale wrinkled face.

Carla left the room and came back a few seconds later. "Daniel is on his way," she mouthed.

Sara nodded her appreciation. Time passed by slowly. She watched the paramedics conduct their job with ease and compassion for the patient.

Ten minutes later, Daniel came into the room and crouched in front of Mrs Strong. "Cilla, I'm so sorry."

Cilla glanced up and reached for his hand. "They've gone, both of them. I hope they're reunited soon."

"This is why I couldn't tell you Linda was missing. You understand, don't you? Can you forgive me?"

Cilla placed a hand on his cheek. "I can. You did the right thing. We didn't think so at the time, but it's clear you were thinking of us. What am I going to do without them?" she wailed.

Sara's heart thundered against her ribs. Her chest ached, and her head filled with memories of three years before, when she'd lost her loving husband.

Carla left her seat and came to stand beside her. She understood what Sara was going through, the trauma the situation had brought to the fore once more.

Sara looked up, tears welling up, and nodded. "It's okay. Is there anything else we can do for you?" she asked Cilla and Daniel.

"No, nothing. I'd like you to leave me and Daniel alone now, if you don't mind?"

"Of course. I'll leave you a card. Give me a call if you need anything at all. You have our sincere condolences."

"I will. Please, promise me you'll do what you can to find Linda's killer."

"You have my assurance. I promise you."

Daniel walked them to the door. Again, Sara felt the need to apologise. "I'm sorry. We broke the news as delicately as we could."

"I don't blame you. Their health was at the forefront of my mind and why I kept them out of this. I hate to be proved right."

"I know. Take care of her, we'll be in touch soon."

Sara and Carla left the house and returned to the car. The second the door was shut, Sara's head hit the steering wheel, and she broke down. "Sorry, the pressure is too much, I have to get it out of my system."

Carla rubbed her back. "I understand. If it's any consolation, I think you handled things exceptionally well in there."

Sara sat upright and leaned her head against the headrest. "What a despicable outcome. Shit! What is going on here, Carla? Another case of a victim well-loved. If she was that popular, why on earth would someone set out to kill her?"

"If that's what happened."

"You think she was in the wrong place at the wrong time? I think we need to be aware of that scenario, yes. We're going to have to speak to the two friends now, I'm guessing." Sara blew her nose on a tissue and wiped the mascara away from under her eyes with another one. "They should be able to tell us more if they were the last to see her alive. Have you got the first address for me?"

Carla gave her the postcode which she tapped into the satnav. "Let's hope they're home."

As it was, both women were out, presumably at work. It took them a little while to find a neighbour at each location who could give them the relative information about where the two women worked. Sara parked the car across the street from the pharmacy where Mandy Cummins was thought to work.

A brunette in a white coat approached the counter and smiled. "Hello, how may I help you?"

Sara produced her ID. "I'd like to speak with Mandy Cummins if possible?"

"Oh, I see. She's out back dealing with a delivery. Take a seat in the corner, I'll get her for you."

Sara and Carla moved to one side and waited.

A few moments later, a blonde woman with a ponytail sought them out. "Hi, I'm Mandy, you wanted to see me?"

"Is there somewhere private we can go to have a brief chat with you?"

"I'll check with my boss, see if it's okay to use his office." She left and returned soon after. "It's fine, come with me."

They passed the till area and walked into an office which was surprisingly tidy, considering its size.

"Do we need to sit down for this?" Mandy asked.

"You go ahead. We're fine."

Mandy sat behind the desk and ran a hand over her face, pushing back a few stray hairs. "How can I help?"

"First of all, I have some bad news for you."

"Oh no, it's not one of my parents, is it?"

"No. This is to do with a friend of yours. Linda Strong."

"Linda? Oh God, is it to do with her going missing? It is, isn't it? Daniel rang me the next day, and I've been trying non-stop to contact her. Is she all right?"

"Sorry to share the news like this…no, your friend's body was found this morning."

Mandy's gaze darted around the room as shock set in, then she wailed, "No, this can't be true. Not Linda, not my darling friend Linda."

"You're aware she went missing on Wednesday evening. Daniel told us that you and Darla were the last people to see her. Would you mind running through the events of that evening with us?"

She buried her head in her hands and cried. "Oh my God, I can't get my head around this." She dropped her hands and asked, "Why her? How?"

"We're unsure how, just yet. At what time did you last see her?"

"Around tennish, maybe a little later. We had an early meal in town and then went to the cinema. Darla and I walked her to the taxi rank at Tesco. She got in a cab, and that's the last we saw of her."

Carla jotted down some notes and looked up to ask, "Can you give us a description of the driver?"

"No. I didn't even take any notice of him. Bugger, you think he did this to her?"

Sara shrugged. "We're unsure at this moment, until we know more facts about the events of that night. Do you recall what colour car it was?"

Mandy shook her head, and a large tear dropped on her cheek during the movement. She wiped it away with the sleeve of her white coat. "No. It was dark. I couldn't tell you. I could guess but what use would that be to you?"

"It's fine. We'll ask around at the rank, see if anyone remembers picking her up. Were you aware of any problems she had in her life?"

"No, there was nothing, not as far as I know. She was happy with Daniel, they were making plans for their wedding. They rarely argued, if that's going to be your next question."

"It was. Okay. Other friends and fellas, anything suspicious there we should know about?"

"Nothing. She was a bubbly character, she drew people to her, instead of pushing them away." She sighed a shuddering breath.

"Are you all right? Can I get you a drink?"

"All right? No, I don't think I'll ever be the same again, knowing that Darla and I were the last people to see her alive and maybe could have prevented her from…dying. My God, why would anyone want to kill Linda?"

"I recognise how hard all of this is for you, but if there's anything you think we should know that would help us with our investigation…"

Mandy stared at the floor for a while and then shook her head. "Not a bloody thing. Her life has been the same as normal. If she was in any trouble, she would have confided in either me or Darla. You'll have to ask her if she can think of anything because I can't, and that's what's frustrating the hell out of me. It's as if I'm letting Linda down a second time by not remembering something important."

"Please, don't punish yourself like that. You've been really helpful telling us where she caught the taxi. That's a lead we didn't have before we spoke to you. You haven't let her down. You took her to the taxi rank believing she would get home safely."

"Yeah, we did. Maybe we should have rung her to check. Or called her yesterday perhaps. I know I didn't think any more about it. Work was full-on yesterday, I worked later than I usually do. By the time I got home I was shattered. I picked up fish and chips on the way, scoffed that and went straight to bed. Why didn't I check on her?"

Sara took out a card and placed it on the desk beside Mandy. "I'll leave you a card. Get in touch if anything comes to mind once we've left. I'm sorry for your loss."

"Thanks. God, how's Daniel taken the news? Stupid question, I know. Bloody hell, what about her parents? Shit! They're both ill, this could kill them."

Sara blinked away the tears. "Daniel seems to be coping, he's at a loss to know why someone would kill Linda. We've just come from breaking the news to her parents."

"And? I'm not liking the way you said that."

"Sadly, her father had a heart attack and died."

Her hands covered her face, and Mandy broke down again. "Jesus, what a cruel world we live in when something like this happens on our doorstep. Poor Linda and her dad."

"I agree. It's unforgiveable. We'll do our very best to find the person responsible, I promise."

Mandy stood, wiped her eyes on a tissue from her pocket, and then showed them back to the pharmacy.

"Take care, Mandy. Again, I'm very sorry for your loss."

"Just get whoever has done this to her, please."

Sara nodded, and she and Carla left. "Shit! Why is this job so damn difficult at times?"

"I know this is proving a tough case for you. Are you sure you don't want someone else to handle it?"

Sara opened the car and got in. "No. I'll be fine. I've got to get past what happened personally and concentrate on the victim. Why kill her? What could she have done to someone that was so bad for them to strip her of her last breath?"

"Your guess is as good as mine. It has to be a one-off. A taxi driver? We need to check that out, don't we?"

Sara blew out a breath. "Yep, how many bloody taxis use that rank at night, though? We don't even know the colour of the car or make, come to that."

"All's not lost, we still have Darla to see yet."

"Yeah, I know. I'm not holding out much hope there."

Sara's prediction proved to be right. Darla cried the whole time they spoke with her. Her mumbled responses were mostly incoherent. She was far too upset to give them anything concrete to go on. So they gave up and left.

"Where to now?" Carla said once they were back in the car again.

"The school. Let's see what the head has to say. This bloody case is taking a toll on me already, and it's only just bloody begun."

"Likewise. I hope we catch a break soon. We could sodding do with one. Want me to contact the station, see what the team can find out about the taxis?"

"Good thinking. Get either Will or Craig to request the CCTV footage around that area, if there is any. There should be, right? It's a supermarket car park."

Carla put the call in to set the wheels in motion.

## 5

***L***ossworth Primary School was quite small compared to others in the area.

The receptionist greeted them with a smile and a frown. "Can I help you?"

Sara flashed her ID. "DI Sara Ramsey and DS Carla Jameson. We'd like a word with the head, please."

"I see. In connection with what?"

"It's personal." Sara grinned.

"I'll ask her if she has time to see you." The woman in her fifties left her desk and disappeared into a room behind her. She emerged a few moments later with a younger woman.

"Hello, I'm Heidi Vickers, the headmistress. What's this about?"

"It would be better if we spoke in private, Miss Vickers."

"It's Mrs. Come this way."

She slipped into the room she'd exited a few seconds earlier, and Sara and Carla followed her.

"Take a seat. I'm intrigued to know why you're here, Inspector. Have I done something wrong? If I have, I'm not aware of it."

"No, it's nothing you've done, Mrs Vickers. I have some sad news for you."

"Go on."

"This morning a member of your staff was found murdered."

"What? Who? No, don't answer that, I think I know who. Linda Strong, right?"

Sara confirmed with a brief nod. "Yes. We're making enquiries into her background and wondered if you'd be able to help us."

"Oh my. I'm sorry, I need to let this news sink in first. I tried calling her yesterday, I wondered why she wasn't getting back to me. Damn. Murdered you say?"

"Yes. We can't give you any other details than that at this time. No doubt the press will report the findings soon. A PM is being performed as we speak. I refuse to give a cause of death until I've read the official documentation."

"I understand. Poor Linda. She was a very special teacher. All the pupils adored her."

"Did she ever come to you with any problems? Maybe in the last few months?"

"No, not that I can recall. Goodness me, this news has shocked me to the core. Can you tell me when it happened? Not that it would make any difference."

"We believe it was possibly Wednesday or maybe Thursday. Apparently, she went out socialising with friends until tennish on the Wednesday and then got a taxi home. No one has laid eyes on her since. Her body was discovered in a lay-by out in the country, miles from her home."

"I see. Was she being stalked by someone perhaps?"

"We could be dealing with a number of possibilities. We're keeping an open mind on things at present. What we're desperate to find out is if Linda has had any unpleasantness in her life of late."

"As far as I'm aware, no, but I must add a word of caution. We weren't really that close that she would feel comfortable confiding in me about personal matters."

"Okay, that's fair enough. What about professionally? Was every-thing going well for her at school?"

"Yes, things couldn't have been better."

"How long had she worked here?"

"Around thirteen years. Just a moment, I'll get her file out." She crossed the room and returned with a file from the cabinet in the corner. She flipped it open and tapped the page with her finger. "Yes, thirteen years in August."

"Perhaps you can tell me if you've ever had a complaint against her, something along those lines?"

"I don't think so, let me check." She leafed through the pages. "No, I didn't think she had."

"That's great. Thanks for the confirmation. And you were satisfied with her work?"

"Extremely. She was the best teacher we had. I'm not sure how I'm going to be able to fill her shoes, if I'm honest."

"Sorry to hear that. What about the other members of staff? Did she ever fall out with any of them?"

"No. Linda wasn't the type. She was the ultimate professional who put the children's interests first, always. She worked tirelessly to make their life experience while at school a memorable one. She was always working at home in the evening, coming up with different ideas to educate the kids in a way that was exciting and challenging at the same time. That's the type of character she was, always putting others' needs before her own. At least, that's the way it came across to me. I can't believe she's gone, not Linda. She was only young." She stared at the file and tapped it again. "Yes, thirty-three, no age at all. She had so much to look forward to as well. What with her impending marriage and the plans she was putting in place for that. Could an ex have had a grudge against her, do you think?"

"We'll be delving into that possibility soon. She sounds like a lovely lady."

"She was. One of the best people I've known, that's for sure, although, I always try to maintain a professional etiquette at work. I'm not one for poking my nose into the staff's personal business. I have enough to contend with as it is without opening my door every five minutes to listen to the staff let off a bit of steam."

"So, even if something was troubling her, she wouldn't be likely to come to you with her anxieties anyway, is that what you're telling me?"

"Sadly, yes. I'm sorry if that sounds a bit harsh. I didn't mean it to come across that way. You see, we're all under pressure to perform, to maintain, if not improve, our standards each year."

"For your governing body?" Sara asked, understanding the pressures of what working against targets meant.

"Yes, and the government set tight guidelines as well. Gone are the days when teachers showed up and sat at a desk at the front of the room and let the pupils work from a text book all day long. It's all about interacting with the children now. Seeing to their different needs, ensuring no one lags behind."

"Thank you for clarifying that. We're always forced to stick to targets, too. I admit, it's a huge bugbear for us to deal with. Okay, if there's nothing else you can tell us then we'll be off."

Sara rose from her seat, and Carla flipped her notebook shut and did the same.

Mrs Vickers saw them to the door. "I'll give her other half, Daniel, a call to express my condolences."

"I'm sure he'd appreciate that. It's been a tough day on the family in more ways than one."

"Oh, how so?"

"Whilst breaking the news to her parents, Linda's father suffered a heart attack and died too."

Mrs Vickers gasped and covered her mouth with her hand. "Oh my Lord, how dreadful for her mother, losing both of them on the same day like that. Was he ill?"

"Yes, both her parents were in ill health. We're hoping this trauma won't affect Linda's mother. We left her in Daniel's care."

"Thank you for letting me know. I'll organise a collection for the family."

"I'm sure they'd appreciate that. Will you call me if you hear of anything you think we should know about rattling around the staffroom?" Sara handed her a card.

"Of course I will."

They walked down the corridor, their shoes smacking noisily on the tiled floor.

"Another waste of time, or so it would seem," Sara grumbled.

"Something doesn't add up, not unless we take into consideration that she might have been in the wrong place at the wrong time. Nothing we've heard about Linda is making me think she has done anything wrong to warrant someone knocking her off."

Sara opened the car door, slipped into the driver's seat and started the engine. "Back to the station then. I'll chase up the PM once we're there. Maybe that will give us something to go on. Because, apart from the taxi angle, let's face it, we've got nothing else."

The incident room was filled with the sound of fingers clacking on the keyboards when they arrived.

"Hi, guys. Has anyone managed to find out anything? We're hoping you've had better luck than we've had out there today."

Will raised a hand, and Sara drifted over to his desk.

"Anything, Will?"

"I've got the CCTV footage. I'm going over it now, boss."

"Good, let me see what you have, when you find it."

"Roger that."

"Anyone else got anything?"

Carla breezed past her and headed for the vending machine. She returned carrying two cups and placed one on the desk next to Sara.

"Cheers, partner."

"We're still digging," Christine shouted from her desk. "There are around two hundred registered taxis in the area."

"Bugger, that's too many to look up. Let's hang fire on that and see what Will comes up with first. I'll be in my office."

She picked up her cup and sat behind her desk, sifting through the mail she'd neglected to get around to opening first thing that morning. She placed the envelopes in the relative piles and sipped at her coffee in between. Once that was out of the way, she called Lorraine, hoping she would have completed the post-mortem by then. "Hi, I'm glad you answered, can you talk?"

"To whom am I speaking?"

"Get you. Don't mess with me, woman."

"Ah, it is you, my dear friend, and the usual daily pain in my arse."

Sara laughed. "What a compliment, I'll take that. It's a mighty fine arse you have, too."

"Bollocks, it's as flabby as hell, just like the rest of me. You're too nice to say that, though, right?"

"Nailed it. Back to work... Please tell me you've finished the PM on Linda Strong?"

"I have, this minute, in fact."

"And?"

"And, I'm on my way to the office to retrieve the file. I was going to have another read through before I despatched it to you. I use this dictation technology to type up the files, and sometimes the words go askew, if you get my drift."

"I do. Not a great fan of it myself. I've heard you spend more time correcting the mistakes. Might as well do it the old-fashioned way."

"It's all about the training. I've been using it a while, so things are gradually improving. I'm here now. Right, what I can tell you is the cause of death was drowning."

"Okay, we kind of figured that, didn't we? Anything else?"

"Obviously she was moved to the location where she was found today. I sent a sample of the water found in her lungs off to the lab, asked them to analyse it as a matter of urgency, and the result came back showing there was some form of oil residue found in the water."

"I see. And how are you interpreting that?"

"She died in water where someone has possibly dumped oil lately. Might be worth getting in touch with the local Environment Agency. To see if they've had any illegal oil dumps in any of the rivers in the area in the past few days."

"I'll get on to that. Anything else? Signs of sexual intercourse?"

"No, nothing like that. I'm sorry I can't give you more. I think the oil is a significant detail, though, at least I hope it will be for you."

"It's better than nothing, I suppose. We're struggling with this one, I can tell you."

"Don't be so hard on yourself, it's early days yet."

"I know. Shit, I forgot to tell you. We went to inform the parents, and the father died in front of us, a bloody heart attack."

"Holy shit! What a shock for you."

"More of a shock for his wife to contend with. Now she's got two bloody funerals to sort out, poor woman."

"What a bummer! We're still running further tests. I'll get back to you if I find out anything else. I'm going to read through this and then send it to you."

"Thanks, you're a star. Oh, one last thing, Linda Strong jumped in a taxi the night she went missing, so we could be looking at a taxi driver as the lead suspect. We're trawling through the CCTV footage now."

"Good luck. Studying the statistics, which I was doing only last week, as it happens, you'd be surprised as I am to know how many cab drivers turn out to be murderers. Definitely something to bear in mind."

"Really? Right, I will do. Thanks for the heads-up. Send it over when you can."

"It'll be with you in no more than twenty minutes."

"Thanks, Lorraine." Sara ended the call and glanced out the window at the angry clouds gathering overhead. Her thoughts drifted to the Strong family and the losses they had incurred in the past couple of days. It made her want to reach out to her own parents. Her father had recently had an operation on his heart. She called her parents' number.

"Hello, who's that?" her mother asked.

"Hi, it's only me, Mum. How are you both?"

"We're fine. It's unusual for you to ring during the day, love. Everything all right?"

"Tough case. I needed to hear a friendly voice. What are your plans for today?"

"Nothing much. Your father is out there tending the seedlings he planted last week."

"He's not overdoing it, is he?"

"No, I'm making sure of that. He's pottering around. I'll help him plant the veg patch this year, don't you worry. How are things coming along with the wedding?"

"So-so, Mum. Mark's whisking me away for the weekend to look at a stunning venue we've found."

"How exciting. Am I allowed to ask where?"

"No. It's top secret for now. Anyway, it might not come to anything."

"Well, enjoy your weekend. I'd better go now, dear, your father's waving frantically for me to join him."

"No problem. Love to both of you. I'll ring you as soon as I can."

"Drive carefully."

"I will." She ended the call and smiled. She couldn't help wondering if she and Mark would resemble her parents in years to come, or even if they'd be together then. *Of course we will, what's to stop us?*

Sara joined the rest of her team and informed them of the PM results. She tasked Marissa with ringing the Environment Agency to see what they had to say about any illegal dumping of oils in the surrounding rivers lately.

Marissa reported back with a negative less than ten minutes later. "So, where does that leave us?" Sara enquired.

The team mostly either shrugged or shook their heads, except for Craig.

"Go on, Craig, what are you thinking?" Sara asked.

"Could we be looking at a chemical plant of sorts? A possible warehouse maybe? A petrol station even? Although suggesting all those places, I'm struggling to think why there could be water on site. Oil residue yes, but water?"

"Well, at the moment it's all we've got to go on. So let's poke the stick and see where it leads us."

"I'll do some digging, boss."

The rest of the afternoon consisted of just that, the team carrying out their respective research, hoping that something would show up to get the investigation underway.

Before knocking off for the evening, Sara paid DCI Carol Price a visit to apprise her of what they were up against.

In instances such as this, every now and then, Price came up with a gem of an idea of where to try next. Unfortunately, things didn't quite pan out that way this time, though.

"It's a puzzling one. I'm sure you and your team will pull something out of the bag soon. What about the taxi driver angle?"

"I'm not relishing seeking out every taxi firm in the area, to be honest. Will's looking at the CCTV now. I'm hoping he'll come up with something soon to help us. Other than that, we're up shit creek and paddling against the bloody rapids."

"It's unlike you to give up so early in the game, Sara. Is there something else on your mind?"

Sara pointed at her. "I know what you're thinking, and no, the wedding plans are not interfering with my work."

"I wasn't insinuating anything of the kind. It's just that it must be rather distracting."

Sara shook her head. "Not in the slightest. May I remind you that I put my plans on hold to find your friend's daughter recently? I didn't hear you spouting this crap when I was investigating Laura Tyler's abduction."

Carol growled. "All right, you've got me there. It was only an observation. There's no need to tie yourself up in knots about it, Inspector."

Sara chuckled. "I wasn't aware I was. Right, I've brought you up to date. Now I'm going to bid you good evening and take off for my dirty weekend, if that's all right with you?"

"Too much information. Have fun, don't get into any trouble while you're away."

"I'll heed that piece of advice. See you on Monday."

The second she returned to the incident room, Will gestured for her to join him. "What is it?"

"Sorry it's taking so long, there was a problem with the disc, it kept stopping at a certain point. Took me a while to figure it out. But here are the results."

Sara leaned in closer to watch the darkened screen. "Yes, those are the three women. Right, it's a dark car Linda is getting into."

"We're doing well up to here. This is where things seem to go Pete Tong. As the car pulls away, someone walks in front of the camera, and the number plate is obscured." He heaved out a sigh.

"Shit! Not what we wanted at all. Hang on, take it back, all is not lost." She pointed at the side of the car. "There you go. Can you pull that into focus?"

"I'm getting where you're coming from. Let's see what I can do to tweak it. Yes, here we go." Will jotted down the number etched on the side of the cab. "I'll give them a ring now."

"You do that. I was about to shoot off, but this is worth hanging around for, I hope."

She raised her crossed fingers, and he placed the call to the cab company.

Rather than standing around waiting for the results of the conversation Will was having, she drifted into her office to tidy her desk.

Will rapped on the door a few minutes later. "I've got the name of the driver. Bad news, though."

Sara threw herself into the chair. "Go on, surprise me."

Will tutted. "The guy dropped Linda off at home and immediately got a call from the cab office to pick up another fare. The timeline is dictating that he wouldn't have had time to either kill her or abduct her."

"There's no way he could have called back later? Or is that me grasping at a bloody bundle of straws?"

"Possibly. The guy finished his shift at two in the morning. Want me to go out and interview him?"

"There's no rush. I'm getting the feeling it would probably be a waste of time. Thanks, Will. Call it a day, and we'll rethink things on Monday."

"I don't mind working extra tonight."

"No, don't bother."

"Okay." His head dropped, and he walked out of the office.

Sara thumped her clenched fist on the desk, and several loose items jumped up in the air. *That's it, it's time to go home. I've had it for the day.*

# 6

*H*e left the house at around four-thirty and travelled to the location in a different vehicle to the one he used last time. Aware of the use of ANPR cameras and CCTV footage available to the police in the area, he needed to be cautious. It wasn't a problem for him, he could get his hands on several vehicles at a moment's notice.

The woman left the large official building. The façade was as grey as the clouds overhead. A storm was brewing, he could sense it, in more ways than one. She hopped into her car. He chuckled at the joy etched onto her face and knew fear would replace it soon enough. He followed her through the town to her home address out at Callow. He remained behind her at a steady speed, ensuring there were at least two cars between them at all times. They rose to the top of the steep hill and indicated right. Luckily, one of the cars in between also took the same route. They were out in the countryside now, going through the winding lanes.

Not far to go.

The other car took a left at a junction up ahead, and the woman chose to go right. He delayed trailing her until she turned the bend in the road then he took up the hunt once more. That's what it was, a hunt, a game to him. He enjoyed the thrill tickling his spine.

Her house wasn't far then, about half a mile or so. A cunning plan seeped into his head. He put his foot down on the accelerator, changing his mind about keeping his distance. Her car came into sight.

He got closer. Closer. Closer.

*Bang*!

His gaze met hers in her rear-view mirror. She shook her fist at him but travelled on. Their bumpers connected once more. She slammed on the brakes, and he did the same. She exploded out of her car and strode towards him.

Winding the window down, he grinned at her. "Something wrong?"

"Are you bloody insane? Look at the damage you've caused."

His hand covered his chest. "My, oh my, I did that? Are you sure?"

She stared at him, her mouth hanging open. Suddenly, her eyes widened as the recognition set in.

Before she had the chance to run back to her car, he leapt out, grabbed her and placed the handkerchief over her face. Her arms and legs flailed less as the chloroform worked its magic. His pride swelled. He'd made up the concoction using a site on the Net, and he was incredibly pleased with the results. Of course, he'd tested it on a few rats during the process, so he had perfected the final product before having to use it on his victims. Again, this left him safe in the knowledge that the police couldn't trace him or where the product likely came from if they suspected its use to abduct the two women so far.

He threw her in the back of his car and drove her to the same warehouse he used to keep the first victim until he got rid of her. His intention had been to make them all suffer for days, torturing the shit out of them. However, being in a confined space with these evil no-marks had riled him to the point where the red mist had descended sooner than he'd anticipated. The conclusion inevitable.

It didn't matter either way to him, the end result remained the same.

He arrived at the warehouse and dragged the woman out of the back of the car and slung her over his shoulder. She was still out cold. This one was a few pounds heavier than the first. He tied her to the seat. Yes, he would use the same method to torture her with a significant twist at the end for good measure.

After securing her to the seat, he dipped his hand into the water and flicked the woman's face. It took a while for her to recover completely; he had the time to wait. He had no plans, no one at home waiting for him. This woman, and the others he had on his hit list, had seen to that. The evil witches. Interfering busybodies. Was that an essential requirement for their jobs? The thought had often drifted into his mind. Maybe he'd get the chance to ask her.

"Please, why are you doing this to me?"

"Because I can. Next question? Nah, don't bother. You talk a lot of shit anyway, you always have done."

"I haven't. If I've offended you in the past, I'm sincerely sorry."

"Are you? How sorry? Enough to alter your decision? To take back your findings in your reports? Revoke everything you've ever said about me, most of which was your wretched perception of me, all of it wrong, I hasten to add?"

"If I have to, yes. I'd be willing to do that."

"Except it's far too late to alter things, isn't it? You're aware of that, aren't you? All you're trying to do now is save your own skin. Go on, admit it."

"I'm not. I can alter things. We're all entitled to have a change of mind in our jobs. I can fight your corner for you. If you'll allow me to. Let me go, and that's exactly what I'll do for you. It's not too late, it's never too late to right the wrongs in this world. Release me, and I'll prove that to you."

"You're unbelievable. This is the most you've spoken to me in over two years. Usually, every time I've contacted you in the past, your response has been clipped and to the point. Denying me..."

"I was wrong. I admit that now. Give me the chance to correct things. To make things better for you and..."

"Go on. You can't even remember his name, can you? And you expect me to believe a bloody word that comes out of your sodding mouth?"

"I deal with a lot of cases, day in, day out. Of course I don't remember all of their names, I'd have to be superhuman to be able to do that. Please, let me make things right. Don't hurt me."

"It's too late. This world will be better without the likes of you in it interfering in other people's lives. You're evil in the purest form. You were given special powers to help people and all you succeeded doing in most cases, I'm guessing, is make people suffer. To tear families apart. Well, that ends today. Your own life ends today. You hear me?"

"No, you don't have to do this. Give me twenty-four hours to put things right for you."

"Why should I? You've had twenty-four months of tearing my life to shreds and you reckon you can rebuild it again within a day? You know what they say? Words are cheap. Even in your dying moments you're making promises you could never uphold." His hand connected with her cheek.

She cried out in pain, her head twisting viciously from one side to the other.

"I'm sorry. I can't emphasise that enough. Let me go, and I *will* make everything right."

"Bullshit! I've listened to the drivel you and your sort have dished out over the years, and seriously, it concerns me how you guys sleep at night. You know when was the last time I had a decent night's sleep, free from nightmares? Two years ago."

"I'm sorry about that. Have you been to the doctor for help? I know someone who could fit you in today. Please, let me help you, make amends for the pain I've caused you."

"It's too late. No one can help me. Retribution is on the cards now, for all of you concerned in this decision. You cannot be allowed to put another soul through so much upset and turmoil any longer. Who gave you the right to be the one to pull the trigger? Treating people like they are worthless pieces of shit? Yes, there might be men out there worthy of what you've done to them, but not me. I work seventy to eighty hours a week, for what? To finish work and sit in the house alone because people like you have robbed me of the family I once had?"

She sobbed, snot mixing with blood, dripping from her nose. "Is there nothing I can say to change your mind?"

He shook his head and lowered her slowly into the oil drum. She kicked out and raised her chin, trying to escape the water, until finally she was totally immersed. He wanted to punish her more than the first one. He would toy with her for a few minutes longer, taking her to the brink of death each time. He pulled on the chain, raising the seat again.

She coughed and gasped for breath. "Please...don't do this. I can help."

"Lady, I'd keep that gob of yours shut if you know what's good for you, you'll only make matters worse."

"Worse? How can things get any worse than you trying to kill me? I was doing my job, that's all. Don't punish me for dealing with the system. It's the system you need to blame, not me."

"Really? You were the one writing up the reports. You ignored everything I ever told you. I gave you an insight into what went on behind closed doors, and you just shrugged it off. She did nothing all day long. I worked from eight in the morning until seven at night most days. Came home to find her sitting on the sofa. My kid playing in the dog cage along with Buster, his nappy soiled, and you chose to ignore that. What kind of insensitive, corrupt person are you? What would it take for you to have listened to me?"

"I'm—"

He cut her off by dunking her into the ice-cold water again. She emerged a few seconds later, grappling for air to fill her lungs. He allowed her a few more seconds to recover and then lowered her a third time. He crossed the room and picked up the old toaster he'd found. He plugged it into the small generator he had set up and dangled it near the edge of the drum. The bubbles covered the water. He stared down at her, her eyes wide with fear, pleading for his help and no doubt his forgiveness by now. He couldn't give a shit, just like she hadn't over the months he'd tried to reach out to her.

He grinned and threw the toaster into the drum. Her body juddered, sparks flew, and then there was nothing except the sound of the wind blowing through the gaps in the warehouse where the windows used to be. Another one down. The elation ran through his veins for a few minutes. Staring down at the woman for a couple of moments longer, the elation gave way to remorse. He shrugged it off. There was no time for any kind of emotion, he had work to do. More people to punish. But first, he needed to get rid of the body.

He had it all worked out. The corpses would be scattered across the county, lying there, waiting to be discovered. He'd be sure to leave no clues apart from the obvious one for the police, that the crimes were all connected. He knew it would take them a while to figure it out. Who he was and why he'd been forced to go to extreme lengths. At the end of it all, he'd accept his punishment as a man. Spend the rest of his life in prison. It would be worth it to rid the world of evil do-gooders.

# 7

When the call came in, Carla was snuggled up in bed with Gary. It was their first Saturday off together in a while, what with pressures of work and Gary's willingness to grab as much physio as he could lay his hands on, in order to regain his fitness. He missed being on duty with the guys in the brigade.

Carla groaned, rolled over and answered the phone. "Hello?"

"Sorry to trouble you on a Saturday, Sergeant. I have it on the system to contact you in DI Ramsey's absence."

Carla propped the pillows behind her and sat up. "That's correct. What's wrong?"

"There's been a body found out at Aconbury. In a small copse down there."

"Okay. You'd better give me the postcode. It'll be half an hour or so before I can get there. I take it the pathologist is at the scene?"

"She is."

Carla jotted down the postcode and ended the call. "So much for our day of fun. Sorry, love."

Gary reached out, drew her close and kissed the tip of her nose. "Nonsense. You go. It must be urgent if they've called you in on your day off. Don't worry about me, I'll spend the time in the gym."

She smiled. "Don't go pushing yourself too hard now. Hopefully, I won't be too long, although I'll have to break the news to the next of kin. Jesus, Sara is usually the one who deals with that part. My head hurts just bloody thinking about it."

"You'll be fine. You're more compassionate than you let on."

Carla sniggered and then frowned. "Umm...I'm not sure whether to take that as a compliment or not."

"It was meant as one. Go, shoo!"

"I'm going. Haven't got time for a shower. Maybe we can have one together when I get back."

His eyebrows waggled. "Sounds like a fantastic idea to me."

Carla had a quick wash, dressed and was ready to leave within ten minutes. She ignored her grumbling tummy and headed out to the car. There was no way she'd entertain having something to eat, not if she was expected to be the lead investigator on this one. Sara was absent, so there was no escaping her responsibility this time.

She drove up and down the road a few times until she finally located the right area, after spotting the SOCO van in a small clearing set back from the main road. She got suited and booted and went in search of Lorraine.

"Ah, you've arrived. Not as punctual as your boss, but you're here now."

Carla opened her mouth to protest but shut it again when Lorraine burst into laughter.

"You should know me by now, I do love winding people up. As Sara isn't here to aim at then you'll have to do. Come this way."

"You're nuts. Is it gruesome?"

"I know I am. It's being nuts that keeps me sane and able to do my job. Yep, it's not pleasant. Had breakfast this morning, have you?"

"No. I thought about it for about two seconds then decided against it. Male or female?"

"Female. I think."

"Oh shit! I wish I hadn't asked now."

"I'm teasing. Definitely female. Similar MO with an added bonus regarding this one."

Carla tutted. "Why do you always have to talk in riddles?"

"I wasn't aware I was. Anyway, come, you'll soon see what I mean for yourself."

They trudged through the damp leaves and into the wooded area beyond.

"Why so far back from the road?" Carla asked.

"I can't answer that."

"Who found the body?" Carla searched the area and spotted a couple standing close to the SOCO van.

"Conscientious dog walkers. I told them to wait around for you to arrive. They're getting a tad impatient, so let's make this quick. The last thing we want to do is piss off the witnesses."

"Agreed. Okay, where's the body?"

"She was buried under a pile of leaves. My guys are photographing the scene now. They should be finished soon."

When they arrived, the SOCO team stood back. Lorraine gently uncovered the woman's head. Her damp hair was plastered to her face.

"Is that because of the moisture in the leaves?"

"I doubt it. I'm pretty confident about linking the two crimes."

"So drowning is the cause of death, as with the first one?"

"Possibly. There's something niggling me about this one that I can't quite put my finger on yet."

"Meaning what? She wasn't drowned? She looks the same as the first one to me."

"I have a trained eye for these things. I need to give you my opinion after I cut her open and see what's gone on inside. I will say, however, that I can smell a distinct odour with this victim."

"From the oil residue? Is that what you're saying?"

"Maybe. I think it's more than that, but I'd prefer to let you know in my report rather than spout something here with no evidence to back it up."

"Great. Okay, I'll have to wait and see then. Do you need me for anything else?"

"No. That's it for now."

"Right, I'll go and question the witnesses. Oh wait, what about an ID for the victim?"

"I thought you'd never ask."

"Bollocks, Lorraine, you know I usually leave this shit to Sara. Give me a break, will you?"

Lorraine grinned. "I knew you'd step up to the plate eventually."

Carla rolled her eyes and turned back to retrace her steps through the trees. The couple, who both appeared to be in their forties, were waiting patiently with two golden retrievers sitting beside them.

"Hello, there. I'm DS Carla Jameson. I understand you're the ones who called nine-nine-nine, is that right?"

"Yes. We rang almost forty minutes ago. We weren't expecting to still be here, waiting to speak to someone."

"I'm sorry, sir. I got here as fast as I could. I was at home and—"

"Yes, yes, I don't really want to hear your excuses. What more do you need from us?"

"I'd like a witness statement, if you have the time. I wouldn't want to hold you up, though."

"You would be holding us up. We have company arriving for lunch and need to get back to make preparations. Can't this be done another time?"

*Geez, don't put yourself out, there's only a dead body lying a few feet away. Sod that, right?* "Of course. The written statement can be taken down at a later date. If you wouldn't mind running through how you discovered the body now, I'd appreciate it."

"It was Jacob, he found it, he disturbed the leaves. I apologised to the pathologist when she arrived. I understand the need to keep things as they are at a crime scene."

"Are you a police officer, sir?"

"No, I'm a magistrate, for my sins."

"I see. I won't keep you long. Can you tell me if there was anyone else in this area at the time you found the body?"

"We've discussed it, and neither of us can remember seeing anyone here on the way in. Jacob uncovered the body on the way out. That was almost an hour later. The dogs enjoy a long walk in the morning, we all do, it sets us up for the day ahead."

Carla smiled at the man whose mood appeared to have softened a touch. "And there were no cars leaving the area as you entered?"

"No, not as far as we know. Can we go now? My wife suffers from arthritis, and standing here in the cold isn't doing her much good."

"Of course. If I can take down your details, I'll get an officer to make arrangements to come and see you in the next few days."

"Of course. It's Gerald and Nadine Brady, ten Elm Tree Crescent, Aconbury. Just down the road, we are."

"And your phone number?"

He gave it to her on a business card. "I'm only part-time, anyway. There's a mobile number on there, contact me on that, if you will."

"Excellent. Thanks very much for all you've done today."

"It's fine. I hope you find the person who took that woman's life." He steered his wife and the dogs away in the direction of their car.

Carla returned to the crime scene.

"Any good?" Lorraine asked.

"They were keen to get off. I told them we'd be in touch soon. They didn't see anyone in the area, which is a bummer. Have you got anything else for me?"

Lorraine and her team had uncovered the victim. Her clothes, a skirt, blouse and jacket, were all wet.

"Nothing as yet. No ID to speak of. Not sure how you're going to get on without that, but I'm sure you'll cope."

"I'll do the usual, check with missing persons when I get back to the station. Apart from that, there's not a lot I can do until Monday."

"Monday? Ah, when Sara returns, right?"

"Yeah, unless you've got any suggestions on what I should do in the meantime, with no ID to hand?"

Lorraine shook her head. "Sorry, nope. That's your department. Are you going to ring Sara?"

"I'm not sure. You think I should? They're away for a romantic weekend. Me bothering her with another murder case is only going to sour her mood, isn't it?"

"My guess is that she'd want to know. You know how antsy she gets being kept out of the loop."

"Even so. She's away sorting out more important things at the moment."

"Well...I think she'd want to know. Either way, you're damned if you do and damned if you don't."

"Ain't that the bloody truth?" Carla ran a hand through her hair.

"Go on. Give her a call. Want me to do it?"

"Would you?"

"Of course, although, my take on it is, that it'll be better coming from you."

"Shit! Mark is going to kill me for wrecking their weekend. She's entitled to her time off, like the rest of us."

"Stop talking yourself out of it and do it."

"Okay. I'll go back to the car and do it there. Anything else I should tell her?"

"That the PM report will be sitting on her desk by Monday morning. I know, yep, no rest for the wicked. I'm on duty all weekend. Staff shortages, as usual."

"Damn, and I thought I had it bad. I'll see you soon."

"Take care. Say hi to Sara. I hope you don't interrupt one of their rumpy-pumpy sessions."

"Fuck! Did you have to say that?" Carla trudged back to the car, removed her protective clothing, slung it in the boot, and then jumped in the driver's seat. She hit number three on her phone and inhaled a steady breath to calm her nerves.

"Carla? Everything all right? It's not Gary, is it?"

"No, he's fine. Still tucked up in bed when I left home earlier."

"So, where are you?"

"At another crime scene. I debated whether to ring you or not. I'm sorry to interrupt you, Sara."

"Stop it. You've done the right thing. I'm not a bloody ogre, love. Who's the victim?"

"A woman, no ID. I'm not sure how to progress now. I was hoping you'd give me some guidance from afar."

"It's a toughie, you know that, without some form of ID for the vic. Where?"

"She was found in a small wooded area by dog walkers. I've spoken to them; they saw nothing. No one in sight and no vehicle at the location."

"Was the woman killed there? Or was her body transferred from another location?"

"Lorraine couldn't tell me that. She's under the impression that the two crimes are linked, if that's any help?"

"Okay, at least that's a start. So was the deceased drowned?"

"Yes, although Lorraine thinks there's more to it this time, but refused to commit until she carries out the PM."

"As usual. She's usually cautious until she has the facts to hand. I take it there was no water close by?"

"Not from what I can tell. I'll take a look on Google Maps, see what I can find out. What do you suggest I do now?"

"Do the necessary paperwork then go home. With no ID, wait, possible time of death?"

"Nope, nothing like that. I'll go back to the station for a couple of hours. Check mispers and see what I can come up with. Sorry to ring you, Sara."

"Don't be. Anytime, you know that. This place is beautiful, by the way."

"I'm glad. Fill me in on Monday. Enjoy the rest of your weekend."

"Here's hoping the killer doesn't go on a murder spree within the next forty-eight hours. Speak soon."

Carla ended the call and drove back to the station. It felt odd being there without the rest of the team. There was no point spoiling their weekend if the victim was a Jane Doe, she knew that. She rang the missing persons department. It took a while for someone to answer her call.

"Hello. Missing persons. How may I help?"

Carla explained the situation. The chappie on the end of the phone asked her to wait a moment or two while he checked the system.

"Okay, we've got nothing reported from yesterday, not so far.

Maybe the family members are aware they have to wait twenty-four hours before they can report someone missing."

"Maybe, or the Jane Doe we're dealing with possibly lives alone and no one has realised she's missing as yet."

"That's a possibility as well, I guess. Either way, I'm sorry I can't help you. If anything comes in, do you want me to call you?"

"If you wouldn't mind. Thanks."

Carla ended the call and crossed the room to the vending machine. She shuddered, not liking the lonely atmosphere one iota. She was grateful about one thing, that it was daylight and the sun's rays were filling the room instead of her being there in the dead of night. That would have totally freaked her out.

She played around with a few ideas regarding the victim and wrote down what she knew about the woman, which amounted to very little, on the whiteboard. After a couple of hours mulling over things, she decided to call it a day and made her way out of the building. As she was passing through reception, she overheard an interesting snippet. She waited patiently for the desk sergeant to end the call.

"Did I hear right? An abandoned vehicle was found out at Callow?"

"That's right. A neighbour of the owner of the vehicle said it was unusual. He found it this morning with the door open in a country lane."

"Give me the address. I think this is worth investigating. Call it a hunch. Or maybe it's me clutching at straws because I haven't got anything else to go on."

The sergeant nodded and wrote out the details on another sheet of paper and placed it on the counter for her to collect.

"Thanks, I'll take a drive out there. If it turns out to be a false alarm, I'll go home, okay?"

"Sounds good to me. Good luck."

The sun was blazing through her windscreen, forcing Carla to wear her sunglasses on the ride out to Callow. This was a lovely area to while away a Saturday morning, in her eyes, whether she was caught up in an investigation or not. She arrived at the location to find the car, a white Toyota, parked at the side of the road. She got out to give it the once-over, noting immediately that there was damage to the rear bumper.

Fishing out her phone, she called the station. The weekend desk sergeant answered her call. "Hi, Dan, it's me again. I've arrived to find a white Toyota sitting here. The back appears to have had a recent bump. I'm just having a quick look around now. While I do that, can you run the plate for me?" She snapped on a pair of gloves.

"Of course."

Carla read out the registration number and continued her search. She tried the driver's door. It was unlocked with the keys still in the ignition. What sane owner would do that unless something extreme had happened to them?

"Are you there, Carla?"

"I'm here. What have you got for me?"

"The car is registered to a Sharon Ryman. I'll give you her address and that of the neighbour who called it in. His name is Warren Pickles."

She noted down the information. "Okay, let me see what he has to say and whether there's anyone at Sharon's residence first. I'm not sure what to do about the vehicle, any suggestions? The keys are still in it."

"Lock it up and take the keys with you, maybe give them to a relative if you manage to locate one."

"I'll do that. Right, I'm off. I'll let you know how I get on."

She ended the call, opened the car door, removed the keys from the ignition and peered into the back seat. There she found a handbag. Carla opened it to see if she could locate any form of ID. Tucked into a purse was a driving licence. She was sure the woman in the photo was the second victim. Sighing, she carried both items to her car where she placed them into evidence bags and popped them in the boot. She placed a call to forensics to pick the car up and then drove to the address the sergeant had given her.

The house was one of three in a small hamlet. The thing that puzzled Carla the most was that the vehicle's owner only lived around five minutes' drive away from where her car was abandoned. "So near and yet so far, if this is our Jane Doe," she mumbled and then left the car.

The house she was after was the one sitting in the middle. It was neatly presented with a well-tended garden at the front. Carla glanced in either direction and, with a riot of colour to each of them, wondered if the three neighbours were in competition as there wasn't much to choose between them all on the neatness rating chart.

She knocked on the door but received no answer. She took out the sheet of paper the sergeant had given her and decided to try the neighbour's house, the one who had reported the car.

"Hello there, Mr Pickles, is it?"

"That's right. And you're the police, I take it. I saw you try next door. She's not there, is she? Did you see her car parked down the road? I'm guessing you did."

"Can I step inside for a moment or two?"

"Sorry, where are my bloody manners? Come in. Can I make up for my rudeness by offering you a drink?"

"No, thanks anyway. Yes, I've knocked next door, she's not there."

"Why am I not surprised? Why would Sharon leave her car five minutes down the road and walk home?"

"Could she have run out of petrol perhaps?" Carla asked the most logical question that entered her mind.

"I doubt it. Anyone living this far out of town usually doesn't go lower than a quarter of a tank, in my experience anyway. And her car door was open, why would she do that. I shut it and came back here."

"Okay, I can cross that off my list. Is Sharon married?"

"Yes, Martin is away on a course at the moment. Not sure where. I don't have a contact number for him, otherwise I would have rung him, made him aware of the situation. Poor bloke is going to be livid when he finds out."

"Livid? Why livid?"

"Wouldn't you be if something has happened to Sharon and you're the last person to know? I think he must be due back today. It's Saturday after all. Maybe he stopped off at a mate's on the way home or dropped in to see his parents, again, pure conjecture on my part."

"I'm willing to listen to anything and everything you have to say, Mr Pickles."

He waved a hand. "Call me Warren, hate my surname. It's been like a tonne bloody weight around my neck over the years. I got bullied at school, don't you know? I hate kids, evil critters at times. I hated my time at school more, mind you."

Carla had to resist the temptation to roll her eyes as he went over his life story. "Sorry to hear that, sir. Going back to Sharon and her husband. Martin, you say?"

"That's right. Nice couple, they are. Both of them work for Social Services, they do."

"I see. Is that local?"

"How should I know? I'm presuming it is. You'll need to contact them, won't you?"

"About the car. When did you find it?"

"First thing this morning. I go out to the local shop at first light, or as near as dammit, to get my morning paper. That's when I noticed it in the lane. I tried ringing the bell when I got back and had a nosey round the rear of the house in case Sharon had left the back door unlocked, and nothing. That bugged me, that did, that's why I rang your mob."

"I'm glad you placed the call."

"Good. I thought you might deem it as wasting police time."

"Not at all. The couple, are they likeable? Any arguments between them, that sort of thing?"

"Not that I can recall. I get on well with both of them. What do you suppose has happened to her? It's not like people to leave their car dumped at the side of the road, minutes away from their home, is it?"

"No, I must admit, that does seem odd. Did you notice the keys were in the car?"

"Bugger, no. I should have taken a closer look. I clocked that the back of the car had a bump in it, though. That was new. Sharon isn't the type to drive around with damage like that."

"Thanks, that helps. Is there anything else you can tell me?"

"Such as what?"

"What about strangers hanging around lately, have you spotted any?"

He pondered the question for a while and played with his stubble. "Not that I can think of. We rarely get people out this way. Maybe someone on a ride out in the country now and again, but most of the time it's the locals who drive past, either on the way into town for work or on a shopping trip. Apart from that, it's relatively quiet out here. Another reason why I rang the station, it all seems a little weird to me. I don't think it's a case of me overthinking things either, if that's going to be your next question."

"It wasn't. You did the right thing contacting us. I'll try and get in touch with Martin. I think it's going to be unlikely over the weekend, however, but I'll do my best."

She heard a car draw up outside, and Warren rushed to the window.

"Your luck's in. That's him now. He doesn't look too happy either. I wouldn't be surprised if he had seen Sharon's car and is wondering what the heck is going on."

Carla flipped her notebook shut. "Thanks for your help. I'll go and see him."

She left the house. Her nerves notched up another level. She was sure Sharon was the victim in the woods. Did she have it in her to tell the woman's husband or should she leave it for now, until her ID had been verified? *Shit! Why did Sara have to be away? I haven't got the confidence to go in there and just blurt it out. I should have, I'm a bloody serving officer, but one mistake, and I could destroy this man's life.*

She left the house and approached Martin's vehicle. He was removing an overnight bag from the back.

"Hello, Mr Ryman. I'm DS Carla Jameson. Would it be okay if I had a word with you?"

"About what? I'm busy. I've only just arrived home and I'm desperate to see my wife."

"It's about your wife, sir."

He halted what he was doing and studied her. "Go on. What aren't you telling me? I saw her car back on the road, I need to see what's wrong. She'd never leave it there unattended."

"Shall we go inside?" She swallowed down the lump of emotion that had lodged itself in her throat.

"Why? What's going on? Do you know where she is? What's happened to her?"

Carla was torn. She was in too deep now to back out. "It would be better if we discussed this inside, sir."

He stomped past her and unlocked the front door which he promptly slammed back into the wall behind. "In the lounge. I'll dump my bag in the kitchen and switch the kettle on. You'll have a coffee, won't you?"

"Thanks, that would be great." Carla opened the first door she came to and walked into a spacious lounge, decorated in muted colours and with stylish new furniture that would be more in keeping with a bachelor's penthouse rather than a country cottage. Each to their own. She moved closer to the photos on the wall and was left in no doubt.

Martin joined her a few minutes later. He held out a mug for her to take and gestured for Carla to have a seat. "What do you know? Let me say first that I've tried ringing her since around six last night and got no answer, either on her mobile or the house phone."

"Where have you been?" she replied, doing her best to avoid answering his question.

"On a course for work up in Derby. I'd made arrangements to stay overnight with my parents who live in Matlock, otherwise I would've driven straight home after the course had ended. What do you know about my wife's disappearance?"

"Disappearance? Could she not be visiting friends or something? Why are you presuming she has disappeared, sir?"

"It's Martin, I hate being called *sir*. And my wife wouldn't go off somewhere without informing me. And before you ask, our marriage is as solid as granite, no cracks in it, and no, she isn't having an affair behind my back. So you tell me."

"My apologies. I didn't mean to cast aspersions." Carla placed her mug on the coaster on the table beside her and linked her hands. "S...

Martin, this is hard for me to say, but I was called out to a murder scene this morning and I believe..."

"No! Don't tell me you think it's her? I don't believe it! You must be mistaken."

"The thing is, I don't think I am. Your neighbour called the station alerting us to the fact that your wife's car had been found up the road... I stopped by on the way here and found the key still in the ignition. Is that something she's ever done in the past?"

"No. I saw her car. Her rear bumper, it wasn't damaged like that before I left. That must have something to do with it. I can't believe what you're telling me. Are you sure it's her?"

"I'm pretty sure. If you've been unable to contact her since last night and you're telling me that sort of behaviour is out of character for her and that you haven't been able to reach her via the phone..."

He covered his face with his hands and rocked back and forth on the edge of the chair. "No. This can't be real. It's not happening, not to me, to us. She can't be..."

When Carla accompanied Sara on occasions such as this, she usually took a back seat and let Sara do all the talking. She was sinking fast here, totally out of her depth. She should never have admitted the truth to the man, except, he had a right to know his wife was probably lying in the mortuary by now. *Think! Think, what would Sara say next?*

"Martin, is there anyone I can call to come and be with you?"

"No. I have no relatives in the area, they all live in Derbyshire. Are you sure it's her?"

She nodded. "I'm so sorry. What about Sharon's relatives? Maybe one of them can come over and sit with you?"

"Oh shit! Her mother has just lost her husband to throat cancer. I can't tell her about this, not until I know it to be a hundred percent true. Are you sure?" he repeated, understandably not wanting to accept the truth.

"I believe so. Once the post-mortem has been performed, which should take place today, you'll be asked to identify her body."

"Jesus. You're going to cut her open? Why?"

"If there are suspicious circumstances, then yes, by law, we have to do a PM."

"This is mind-blowing. I come home after a few days away to find my wife has been killed. How the fuck am I supposed to deal with that news? What can I say or do to bring her back? I'd give my life for hers. She didn't deserve to die, not now, not at her young age."

"How old was she?"

"Thirty-one. That's all. No age is it?"

"I have to ask if she had any enemies at all. Someone you think who might have deliberately set out to kill her."

"No, not that I can think of. What about her car? Someone must have shunted her. What if she had an accident and got out of the car to tackle the bastard and he did this to her?"

"It's plausible, I suppose. Was she the type to confront danger like that?"

"She spoke her mind. She would have been angry if someone had banged into her car. I don't suppose she would have held back. I know I wouldn't if a bastard had done that to me. Shit! You hear of this type of thing occurring and think it will never happen to you…and yet, here we are discussing it. I don't want to believe it's her, not until I get proper verification. We've only been married eighteen months. The best eighteen months of my life, I might add, and now, you're telling me she's gone."

"So very sorry for your loss. I know my words aren't enough to bring her back but…"

"You're only doing your job, right?"

There was nothing more she could say. While her sympathies lay with him, she felt overwhelmed by her surroundings and emotionally wrought, enough to want to leave. Purely selfish of her, she realised that, but leaving was a better option than remaining there in an uncomfortable trance.

"I'll leave you a card. If you should need to contact me, please do. The pathology department will be in touch with you shortly. I'll give them your details."

Martin showed her to the door. He appeared stunned and simply going through the motions, which tugged on her heartstrings. Carla said a quiet goodbye to him and walked back to her car and drove away. A mile up the road, she pulled over. The tears came thick and fast as if her emotional dam had finally burst. After several minutes, she gave herself a good talking to and drove back into town. It had been a long week, and she was in dire need of a few days off, but was that all it was?

She doubted it. She'd filled Sara's shoes and hated it. The responsibility and onus on her to carry out a respectful job of breaking the devastating news to a loved one had churned up her emotions way more than she'd expected it to. Instead of returning to the station, she went back home. Gary was up and working out in the spare room on his gym equipment. Sweat poured from his forehead, and his top was now a two-tone blue, wetter in some areas than others.

"Hey, you! Should you be exerting yourself that much?"

"Don't start, Carla. How did you get on?"

She sat on the end of the bench next to him, her elbows digging into her thighs and her head in her hands. "I don't want to do that again in a hurry. It was pure agony, torture even."

"What was?"

"Breaking the news to the husband that we've discovered his wife's body in the woods this morning."

"Shit! Not the type of news I'd relish hearing, that's for sure. How was he?"

"Distraught, but he coped. Me, well, that was a different story. I left the house and broke down in tears a mile up the road."

"Why?"

She turned to face him. "That chore is usually down to Sara to deal with."

"Ah, I get you now." He leaned over and kissed her cheek. "Have you eaten?"

"Nope. I left the house without stopping for breakfast."

"Good. Let me get showered and changed and I'll whip us up a brunch, how's that?"

She smiled and nodded. "You're too good to me."

"I know. Don't forget it either."

He moved his weights to the side and winced when he stood.

Carla reached out a hand to steady him as he toppled towards her. "Hey, are you okay?"

"I'm fine," he snapped and left the room.

She finished the job off for him and went downstairs to get the ingredients out of the fridge. He joined her around ten minutes later, and together they knocked up a full English breakfast which they devoured within minutes.

"What are your plans for the rest of the day?" Gary asked.

"Barring any other calls from the station, the rest of the day is ours. Is there anything you want to do?"

"I need to pop out for a few supplies, the cupboards are getting low, in case you hadn't noticed."

"Ah, I know I'm lacking in the domestic goddess department, sorry."

He placed a hand over hers. "You have a good excuse, you work exceptionally long hours, as today proved. I'm fine. I can go, leave you to chill out here."

"Or I could come and we could go for a walk somewhere. The exercise will do us both some good."

"Deal. We'll go up to Queenswood, we haven't been up there for a while."

"Great." She didn't have the heart to tell him that she and Sara had stopped off there for a quick break a few days earlier. That was totally different to having a wander around the wood itself. "I'll just change into a pair of jeans."

"In other words, you're expecting me to wash up, even though I helped cook the damn brunch."

"You could always leave it until I come down. It might delay us getting out, though." She sighed at yet another one of his mood swinging sessions. She should have done it by now, but it was a real struggle getting used to them.

He picked up a tea towel and flicked her backside as she scampered out of the room.

# 8

Sara trudged her way into the station. She was reluctant to let her weekend go and return to work. She and Mark had thoroughly enjoyed their couple of days away in Scotland on their scouting trip for suitable wedding venues. Now it was back to reality with a bump. Yes, Carla had rung her the moment she'd discovered the body and given her a few updates since, but she had an idea a long day would still be ahead of her once she stepped into the incident room.

"Morning, Jeff. How are we today?"

"We're fine, boss. No need to ask how your weekend went."

He grinned, and her cheeks warmed under his searching gaze.

"Get away with you. Yes, we had fun, and it's definitely on our 'must visit again' list. You ever been to Scotland?"

"Aye, my father used to take me fishing up at Loch Lomond when I was a nipper. Can't say I've ever thought about going up there again. Maybe I'll have a word with the missus about that, although she tends to drag me off to sunnier climes abroad."

"I think I'd much rather stay in the UK than fly these days. I had a bad experience a few years ago which kind of freaked me out."

"You survived it, though! Don't write off going abroad in the future, boss."

"Nothing you or anyone else says could ever persuade me to board another plane, I assure you. Look around this beautiful country of ours. There are hidden treasures to discover in every county, I guarantee it."

"I know you're right. Maybe I'll work harder on persuading my missus to give up her Med tan and exchange it for a UK rusty one instead."

"Are you crazy? Look at the stunning weather we had back in April and the first week in May."

"Aye, but then, I can hear her saying it now, 'Just look at the floods we experienced back in February'."

Sara sniggered and placed her hand on the internal door which Jeff buzzed open to let her through. "Okay, I think she might have a point there. See you later. Oh, by the way, is Carla in yet?"

"Yes, she arrived ten minutes ago."

Sara climbed the stairs and entered the incident room to find the rest of the team hard at work. "Bloody hell, I should go away more often if this is what greets me upon my return."

"I think Carla might have something to say about that," Christine shouted. She ducked when a screwed-up piece of paper came from Carla's direction and missed her head by inches.

The rest of the team laughed, even Carla, after a few imaginary daggers darted in Christine's direction.

"Coffee and post, in that order, and then we'll run through what's happened while I've been away. All right?"

"Sounds like a great idea," Carla replied.

"I take it you want a coffee, right?"

"I would never say no, especially if you're paying."

"Anyone else? Speak now while my generosity is at its peak, it won't last long."

She ended up buying all of them a coffee. Carla helped her to distribute the drinks then left her to it to get on with the mundane task of dealing with head office's mountain of bureaucratic nonsense and frequently changing procedures.

Almost thirty minutes later, she rejoined the team and asked Carla to go through what she'd dealt with on Saturday morning.

"That's about it. I did drop the woman's handbag and keys off to forensics, just in case they could offer any DNA evidence."

"Thanks for dealing with that. I appreciate how far out of your comfort zone that was for you, partner."

Carla closed her eyes and sighed. "Way outside. I don't know how you do it."

"It's hard, I can't deny that. You have to dig deep and switch off your emotions. No, that's the wrong thing to say. Keeping them under control would be a better way of saying it. I'm sure you coped admirably. How did you leave it with the husband?"

"I told him that the pathologist would be in touch after completing the PM. I rang Lorraine in the afternoon. She'd carried out the PM and said she'd be sending over the report today."

"I haven't received it as yet. I'll ring her in a sec, give her a friendly prod. She's of the opinion the crimes are linked, for definite, right?"

"Yep. She seemed pretty confident."

"So, what does this lead us to think? Two victims, both women. Were they initially abducted by chance or intentionally targeted? If the latter, then why?"

Carla shrugged. "Nothing is leaping out at me right now, apart from them being female, that is."

"What job did Sharon do?"

"She and her husband are both social workers."

Sara ran a hand over her face and then jotted the information down on the board. "A primary school teacher and a social worker. Both similar ages, I believe."

"Yep, Linda was thirty-three and Sharon thirty-one," Carla confirmed.

"Okay, could there be something in the background which links them? Did they know one another? If so, how? Through their work or personally? Could they have attended the same school? We need to start the background checks straight away. Look at whether her husband's absence is a legitimate one. Some might call it a coincidence him being away at the same time she goes missing and winds up dead."

Carla raised her hand to speak. "I know we have to check out his alibi, but I'd like to chime in and say that he seems pretty genuine to me. I asked his neighbour if he ever heard them arguing, and he told me categorically that he hadn't."

"How long had they been married, Carla?"

"Only eighteen months."

"Possibly still in the honeymoon period then. Okay, we're going to have to check, all the same. What else do we have?"

Carla shrugged. "Nothing as yet. We're reliant on what the PM has to offer us, aren't we?"

"I'll get on to Lorraine now. One last thing… Sharon's car was damaged. We need to bear that in mind going forward when any suspects come to light. Forensics have the vehicle, do they?"

"I actioned it on Saturday. Want me to chase it up?"

"If you would. Christine, will you look into the bank accounts of both victims for me?"

"Will do, boss."

"Barry, do the usual CCTV searches. Marissa, ring Social Services, get Sharon's background, see if she's dealt with any high-profile cases which could have come back and bitten her in the bum. Craig, I need you to check on Sharon's background, personal, any ex-partners who could have done this. That sort of thing. I'll be in my office."

She walked into the office and closed the door behind her, shutting out the rest of the world, pausing to take in the incredible view of the Brecon Beacons which generally set her up for the day ahead. She continued to her seat and picked up the phone only to find Lorraine was too busy to take her call. "Can you get her to ring me back ASAP?"

"Of course, Inspector," a female lab technician said.

Sara went back to tidying up the paperwork on the previous case they'd solved until Lorraine called back.

"Christ, you took your time, the day's almost over," she joked light-heartedly, hoping that Lorraine wouldn't take offence.

"Cheeky cow. I'll have you know that I've been tied up performing PMs since six this morning. Some of us don't work nine-to-five jobs."

"Ooo…get you. All right, I'll let you off this time. Carla mentioned that you said you'd fling the Sharon Ryman PM report in my direction first thing. I'm still waiting."

"Bloody hell. Was I talking a different language just then?"

"No. Sorry, I'm eager to see the report, that's all."

"Yeah, and I'm eager for a decent frigging shag, but one never seems to drop into my lap as easy when I snap my fingers and expect them to. So that makes us even, right?"

Sara covered the phone and roared. She wiped a tear that had leaked from the corner of her eye. "Touché, I'll give you that one. Sorry you're not getting any hot sex at the moment. Have you ever thought the red hair might be a turn-off for any possible suitors? You know what they say about redheads having a fiery temper."

"Natural redheads maybe. Mine's out of a bottle as well you know, it doesn't count."

"Whatever, just trying to offer you a different perspective on why your minge might have healed over by now."

"What the hell? I'm not even going there. The quicker I get this report sorted out, the quicker I can end this farcical conversation. Now, where's that damn file. Ah yes, here it is. I've typed it all up. I'll scan it and send it over."

"Can I stay on the line so we can discuss it once I receive it—if you're not too busy, that is?"

"If you must. Two ticks."

Sara tapped her pen while she waited. The scanner churned into life on the other end of the line, and then she hit the refresh button on her email until the report finally appeared. "You never asked how I got on over the weekend?"

"Like I've had time to do that. How did it go?"

"Fabulously—"

"Wait, I wasn't talking about the sex, I meant the venue."

"Bloody hell, you've got it on the brain for sure. It's the venue I was referring to. The place is like a mini castle-cum-manor house just on the borders."

"Great, can't wait to see it. Why are you expecting people to travel all the way up there?"

"Not many people are going to be there. It's going to be an intimate gathering, and who said you're invited anyway?"

"Charming, and there was me thinking I would be the first name on your list. Any chance I can cop off with the best man?"

"Doubt it, he's happily married. Keep your eyes and hands off on the day. Ah, here it is now. Come on, back to the job."

"You read it. I'll roughly go through it with you. Although I do think there's a slight connection between the victims, I'm going to throw in a word of caution as well."

"Hang on, let me try and see why that is. Give me a sec to skim-read it."

Lorraine fell silent.

"Bugger, I think I've got it. She didn't drown per se, you think she was placed in water and then electrocuted?"

"Yep, that's my assumption. There was minimal water found in her lungs, not enough to drown her."

"Jesus, why?"

"You tell me. Maybe she refused to die and the killer got fed up with trying to drown her and resorted to more drastic measures."

"Holy crap! What a way to go."

Lorraine cleared her throat. "You think there's a good way to go?"

"No, shit, you know what I mean. To fry like a piece of battered cod must have been just frightful."

"You're nuts. Every death is 'frightful'."

"All right, we've established that for now, maybe it was a bad choice of words."

"No shit, Sherlock. Anyway, how's the investigation going at your end regarding the first victim?"

"Not well at all. Everyone we've spoken to has given us the usual drivel about what a wonderful person she was and how they can't believe anyone would want to hurt her."

"That must be frustrating as hell, hearing the same old crap all the time."

"Yep, it gets a tad monotonous. At least with two victims to deal with we can start digging deeper for possible links et cetera. I've got my team doing their best to find something now. Apart from that, we're getting nowhere fast."

"I'm sure things will slot into place soon, they usually do the more you dig."

"It would be helpful if we had some DNA or other evidence to go on."

"I think forensics are doing their best."

"Carla's chasing them up. They've got Sharon Ryman's car, handbag and keys to deal with. I'm not counting my chickens on them finding anything of note, though."

"Well, you know where I am if you need to talk things over. If I'm not up to my eyes in blood, guts and intestines, that is."

"Thanks, mate. If anything else comes to mind regarding the vics, well, you know the drill, ring me."

"You have my word. Good luck, and I'm glad you had a restful weekend. Something tells me that the next week or so is going to have you stressed out again before too long."

"Just what I wanted to hear, not. Thanks for your wondrous insight."

She ended the call and left the office to see if the team had managed to find out anything.

"What have we got, guys?"

Craig motioned for her to join him. "I've got an ex-husband for Sharon Ryman. I'm searching the database for a current address for him now."

Sara squeezed his shoulder. "Great news. Barry?"

"I've requested the CCTV footage, waiting for it to arrive. I'll get on it ASAP."

"Christine? Anything shown up in the bank statements?"

"Nope, nothing dodgy that I can see. Regular bills listed. She liked to shop in the same stores for food and clothes, and there are a few catalogue payments going out every month."

"Okay, everyone, I need you to keep digging. The women aren't similar in appearance, so I think we can discount that viewpoint. Why is he abducting them and then killing them?"

"I have a thought I'd like to share," Carla announced.

"Speak freely, go on," Sara encouraged with a nod.

"Just something that's been playing on my mind, if you will. Linda Strong's body was recovered two days after she went missing—was that because it was missed? Or did the killer hold her captive for a day or so before he did the deed?"

"Good point. Maybe he was apprehensive about killing her? Suddenly had a touch of conscience and struggled to finish her off?"

"Or maybe he intentionally kept her, tortured her before he decided to end her life. And with the second victim, Sharon Ryman, maybe she angered him in some way that ended her life sooner than he'd antici-pated when he abducted her."

"Possibly. By the way, Lorraine reckons she wasn't drowned, she was electrocuted."

Carla visibly shuddered. "Something was immersed in the water with her? That's sick. Why?"

Sara shrugged. "Any number of reasons. She pissed him off. He's perfecting his skills and upping his game. Time is of the essence, and he could be out there eyeing up his next victim. God, I hope I'm wrong about the last one."

"So do I. I can do without dealing with a bloody serial killer case, although I have to say, the signs are there with the frequency of the two crimes. What else is going to land on our plate soon?"

"It's best not to dwell on it. Thinking about it might mean it comes to fruition, if you get where I'm coming from. Let's try to remain posi-tive and concentrate on finding a link between the two women. In the end, that will hopefully lead us to the killer."

"Fingers crossed," Carla mumbled.

"In the meantime, I think we should go to her place of work, see what we can find out there."

"If I can interrupt, boss," Will shouted over.

Sara crossed the room to his desk. "What have you got, Will?"

"I chased up the husband's alibi first thing, and everything checks out. He was at a conference and stayed at the same hotel for two nights. He left there around five on Friday and travelled to his parents' house. Set off around eight on Saturday to arrive home just before eleven. That's when Carla caught up with him."

Carla nodded. "Yes, it must have been around that time, although I didn't check my watch. I know I should have."

"No recriminations, Carla. You did well, I have no qualms about that." Sara turned back to Will. "Thanks, that makes life a little easier. At least we can discount him for now. He could well be involved and used the time away to give him an alibi. We'll see how that pans out eventually."

"Want me to dig into his past, just in case?"

"Why not? It can't hurt. The more information we can muster about all concerned at this stage, the better. Carla and I are going to head off now. Stick with it, guys. Give us a shout if anything significant rears its head."

Carla grabbed her jacket off the chair and joined her at the door. They left the building and got on the road. The traffic had petered out, giving them a clear route to the Social Services building on the other side of town. MASH as it was known, the Multi-Agency Safeguarding Hub was a run-down building in dire need of a lick of paint on the outside. Inside didn't fare any better either.

"Crikey, and I thought the station was in need of a makeover," Carla murmured as they entered the main entrance.

"I'm inclined to agree with you. This is disgusting, not exactly portraying a welcoming atmosphere for the general public, is it?"

"It's sick, that's what it is."

"Maybe I'll put in an official complaint on their behalf, it might be worth a shot. Anyway, that's by the by for now."

There was an older lady sitting at a reception desk. She saw them approach and pushed her glasses up into her greying hair. "Hi, can I help?"

Sara and Carla flashed their IDs.

"Is it possible to speak to whoever is in charge?" Sara asked.

"May I ask what this is about?"

"A member of your staff. I can't tell you more than that for now."

"I see. I'll give Sandra Duck a call. Give me a second."

Sara and Carla stepped away from the desk while the receptionist placed the call.

Within moments, a woman in her sixties appeared from a door off to their right. She approached them with an outstretched hand. "Sandra Duck, pleased to meet you. How can I help?"

"Likewise. I'm DI Sara Ramsey, and this is my partner, DS Carla Jameson. Is there somewhere private we can discuss what we have to say?"

"In my office. Come through."

Sandra led the way into a large square office, ram-packed with storage boxes from floor to ceiling. "Excuse the mess. End-of-year crap to deal with. I'm sure you know how that feels, right?"

"I occasionally get overwhelmed with paperwork. Nothing to this extent, thank goodness. Are these ongoing cases?"

She sighed heavily. "Afraid so. Still, Gloria mentioned that you wanted to discuss a member of staff with me. May I ask who? Sorry, take a seat, won't you?"

"Thanks."

After they were all seated, Carla extracted her notebook, ready for action.

"Sharon Ryman," Sara said.

"Oh my, I should have known that. I heard the news from Martin this morning. It came as such a shock."

"Is her husband at work today?"

"No. He rang me at home this morning. I told him to take a few days off. Knowing Martin, he'll be back to work tomorrow, and who would blame him? It'll be horrendous for him being at home, dwelling on things, surrounded by memories of Sharon. Well, that's how I would perceive things."

"Maybe you're right. Can you tell us a little about the couple?"

"They were genuinely happy together. Both really nice, caring people, devoted to their work."

"I hear Martin has been away on a course or at a conference at the end of last week, is that right?"

"Yes, he's in line for a promotion. That amounts to him needing to brush up on a few things before he takes on the role. I couldn't be more pleased for him. Neither of them deserved this. Martin told me Sharon had been murdered, is that correct?"

"I'm afraid so. We can't really go into too much detail. The thing is, this is the second murder case that has landed on my desk in the past week; we believe they're connected. Hence our being here. Perhaps you can tell us if she's had any bother at work recently?"

"Have you seen the reviews online for this place? Bother, yes, we're always involved in trouble, none of it any of our making, I have to say. We carry out a job that most people find heartless, borderline corrupt. We're not in the slightest. We have a tough role to contend with on a daily basis. The truth is, we only get involved when people do something wrong. The tables get turned on us, however. We're often being slated in the press as interfering busybodies, when all we're trying to do is protect people, or children, should I say."

"A thankless task, I shouldn't wonder, most of the time."

"Exactly. If someone has deliberately targeted Sharon because of the nature of her work, then I'll be devastated to hear that. We're normal people, trying to make a difference to families in distress. Those who are going through problems, either caused by a breakdown of a relationship or by a change in circumstances, such as losing a job and all that entails, both financially and emotionally. We're here primarily to make people's lives easier. That's not how the general public view us, unfortunately. Maybe the press is to blame for that. The way they come down heavily on us without having all the facts to hand. People in the media are quick to judge, in my experience."

"Sorry to hear that."

Sandra gestured at the stack of boxes. "You can see the pressure we're under. If people behaved themselves and cared for their children properly, there wouldn't be any need for us to get involved. Sadly, that's not the case. We do our utmost to work with families to give them all the best outcome. Nine-tenths of the time that works, it's the other part of that fraction that causes us problems. So, to answer your original question, my response would be to tell you to look through the files and take your pick. Let's just say, being social workers, we're rarely at the top of people's Christmas card list."

"I understand. Maybe if we can whittle it down to any cases that stand out in your mind which have taken place in the past few months?"

Sandra sat back in her chair and glanced up at the ceiling. Eventually, she sat upright again and picked up her pen which she twirled through her fingers. "I would need to go through Sharon's case notes. Nothing is really jumping out at me right now."

"Can you do that while we wait? Sorry to put you under pressure like this, I'm sure you can understand the necessity to get things underway quickly when dealing with a murder inquiry."

"I totally understand. Can you give me ten to fifteen minutes?"

"Of course. Thanks very much."

"No problem. Do you want to stay here? I could get Gloria to make you a coffee while you wait."

"There's no need to put yourself out. We'll stay if it's all right with you?"

Sandra hopped out of her chair as if it had suddenly caught fire beneath her and raced out of the room.

"She seems nice enough. Let's hope she can come up with the goods."

Carla nodded. "And I thought our job was an unappreciated one at times. Not sure I could take on a job working here."

"Sounds mighty tough. I bet their wages don't reflect the amount of hassle they have to contend with either. Makes you value your own job when someone else's problems are laid out like that, right?"

"Yeah, what's that old saying? There's always someone out there who is worse off than yourself."

"Ain't that the truth? Something is telling me we're on the right track being here."

"Your gut instinct telling you that?"

"Yeah. I tend to ignore it most of the time, it's just now and then it prods me with a big stick, making me sit up and listen to it."

Sara's phone rang. She swiftly answered it. "DI Ramsey."

"Sorry to trouble you, boss, it's Craig."

"Not a problem. Have you got something for us?"

"I have. Sharon Ryman's ex-husband's address."

"I'll put you on speaker, just a tick. Right, go on, Carla can take down the details for me."

"Tim Davis, he lives at seventy-eight Greenbank Rise, that's in the Rotherwas area." He also gave her the postcode.

"Thanks, Craig. Once we've finished here, we'll shoot over there to see him. Can you give me anything else on him?"

"Not really. He works as a bus driver. So if he's not at home, you might want to try his work. It's Regional Travel."

"Rightio. Good job. Everything else all right there?"

"Yes, Barry has got the CCTV footage. Want me to help him with that now?"

"If you would. We'll be in touch soon. Ring us if you find out anything else."

"Okey dokey."

Sara ended the call. "We'll go there next. I'll look up the number for the bus firm just in case."

"I've done it already."

"You're too efficient at times."

Carla sniggered. "Is there such a thing?"

"Maybe not."

The door opened, and in walked Sandra Duck again. She placed a dozen thick files on her desk and let out an exaggerated puff of breath. "I need to renew my membership to the gym, I think. There, you see what I mean? All that paperwork to deal with, and people wonder why we have a lot of colleagues off with stress-related illnesses throughout the year."

"Blimey, that's a vast amount of paperwork. I'm curious, why do you continue working here if the pressure is too great at times?"

"Why are you a copper? It gets under your skin, I'm sure you'll agree. Caring what happens to people is our main focus, I guess. We do our darnedest to keep the families together where at all possible, but the families have other ideas more often than not."

"It must be hard for you, dealing with people who dig their heels in."

"It is. We get by most of the time. The odd occasion, maybe more than that, everything blows up in our faces. Right, want me to go through these open cases with you?"

"I might need an extra notebook," Carla grumbled.

Sandra opened a drawer in her desk and took out a spanking new one and dropped it on the desk in front of Carla. "There you go. My gift to you, how's that?"

"Thanks, it's appreciated."

"Right, let's start with this one." She scanned through the notes and then shook her head. "Nope, Sharon has entered a note at the end to say there's talk the family are trying to work through their problems, willing to give it a go. She's intentionally left it open for a few weeks, just in case. That's probably what I would do, in her shoes." Sandra placed the file at the top of her desk and flicked through the second one. Sara was eager to lend her a hand, just to speed the process up, however, there would be no point, she wouldn't know what she was looking for. So accepted the situation as it stood.

Before long, Sandra had created three piles. One for cases already dealt with that remained open. The second pile consisted of possible cases likely to sprout trouble soon. And the third pile comprised of three files where the fathers being investigated for either child neglect or possible abuse had used a threatening tone towards Sharon.

"Our staff are encouraged to be truthful with their reports. Most people might brush off the odd touch of anger shown against them, but I insist on noting everything down...I suppose for when things go wrong."

"If that's what has happened to Sharon, we're open-minded about things at present. But I'm sure what you have to say today will have a significant bearing on the case. Oops, I'm guilty of getting ahead of myself there. I should slot the word 'possibly' in that sentence. Mind if I have a brief look through the files you've highlighted?"

"Go for it. Right, I don't know about you two, but I'm desperate for a cuppa. Are you sure I can't tempt you?"

Sara smiled. "Okay, you've twisted my arm. White coffee, one sugar for me."

"The same for me, thank you," Carla replied. She put her notebook on the desk, and both she and Sara took a file each from the pile.

"I won't be long. The information you need should be easy to locate. Let me know if I can be of help upon my return."

She left the office again, and Sara and Carla flicked through their relevant files. They took it in turns to jot down the important details relating to each individual case. When the case began. How things were proceeding. If there were anger issues. Names and addresses of those concerned. Sara was encouraged by the information they had gathered by the time Sandra came back and handed them their drinks.

"Any good?"

"Maybe. It'll be a start anyway. We've just got one more to do, and that'll be us out of your hair."

"I'll do it," Carla volunteered.

Sara issued a grateful smile and took a swig of her coffee.

"I'm glad to be of help. That poor woman didn't deserve to die the way she did. If her job has anything to do with her death, well…that'll be me rethinking my decision to work here, I can assure you."

"I'm getting the impression you're at the end of your tether."

Sandra picked up her cup and sipped at her drink, pausing before she answered, "Thirty-five years I've given to this job and trying to keep the people of Hereford safe. I refuse to put my life on the line as well as my sanity. It takes its toll on a person's wellbeing after a while, I can tell you."

"I'm sure. I can't tell you that things will change in the future because, let's be honest, no one can predict what the economy will be like a few months, or years, down the line. Who knows what's around the corner for any of us?"

"Precisely. I have a couple of grandchildren knocking around who I'd like to get to know better."

"You mean they live elsewhere?"

"Yes, in Devon. My husband and I go down there when we can, but it's limited when you only get four weeks' holiday off a year from work."

"Maybe you could get a transfer down that way, have you considered that?"

"No, not really. My husband has elderly parents living in Hereford. We tend to put them first in all our decisions."

"That's a shame." Sara liked this woman and felt sympathy for her.

"Never mind. Let's not forget why you're here today. I hope you find something in the files. There again, on the other hand, I'm hoping you don't, because if it turns out one of our clients has done this to poor Sharon, well...you can imagine the uproar that's going to cause with the rest of the staff, can't you?"

"I can imagine." Sara scanned through the final file with Carla, again, noting down the relevant details.

They finished their drinks and Sandra showed them back to the reception area.

Sara shook hands with her. "Thanks for sparing us the time today and for the information as well, it's much appreciated."

"I hope it proves useful. I know you'll do all you can to find Sharon's husband the justice he's seeking now. It was good to meet you both. You have my number, don't hesitate to give me a call if I can be of further assistance to you."

"That's great. Thanks, Sandra. It's nice to meet someone in your position willing to help out with such information. So many people in authority dig their heels in and don their jobsworth hats as soon as we step through the door."

"What good does that do anyone at the end of the day?"

"Precisely. Thanks, see you."

Next, Sara drove to the ex-husband's address. Surprise, surprise, there was no one at home during the day, so Carla rang his place of work while Sara spun the car around and headed back into town.

"Thanks, that's very helpful. We'll drop by soon." Carla ended the call and placed her mobile in her lap. "He's out on a route at the moment. Due to return for a lunchbreak soon, within the next thirty minutes or so."

"Excellent. Makes a change for something to go our way. Want to stop off for a quick sandwich somewhere?"

"Why not? My treat this time."

Sara faced her and grinned. "We'll fight over that when we get there. It was my suggestion, so by rights, I should pay."

"What about a drive-through, the KFC in town?"

"Perfect."

They arrived ten minutes later and ordered two chicken burgers with a portion of fries to share, and two Cokes to wash it all down. They sat in the car park and mulled over what they'd learned that morning as they ate.

"Could it really be someone with a grudge?" Carla took a large bite out of her burger.

Sara toyed with the chips in the cardboard container in her lap. "Why not? If the MO wasn't the same, then I'd be willing to put them down as both women possibly being in the wrong place at the wrong time. They're not, though, are they? So who would want to kill a primary school teacher and a social worker, except if that person was carrying a grudge?"

"Can I make one observation?"

"Go on," Sara urged.

"Both abductions took place close to the victims' homes."

Sara nodded slowly. "He either followed them home or knew where they lived and was stalking them, right?"

"Yeah, that's what I was thinking. Either way, we're on the same wavelength in our assumption that these women were specifically targeted and killed. The only other question we need to seek the answer to is why."

"That's the sixty-four-million-dollar question all right, and I reckon, over the next few days or weeks, that question is going to drive us round the bloody twist. There, that's my prediction."

Carla chuckled and took another chunk out of her burger. They finished their lunch and went in search of the bus company, joining the traffic en route. Sara hated driving through the centre of Hereford. It always seemed to be chocka with traffic, no matter what time of day it was.

## 9

The manager, Mr Phillpotts, showed them into a small room, close to the canteen to give them some privacy. They declined the offer of yet another cup of coffee. He left them and returned a few minutes later with the man they'd come to see, Tim Davis.

"This is Tim. He'll need to eat before he gets on the road again, so if you wouldn't mind making this interview snappy, I think we'd both be grateful to you."

"Don't worry, Mr Phillpotts, we won't take long, I promise," Sara affirmed with a smile.

Tim seemed confused. He watched his boss leave the room and pulled out the chair opposite them and sat with a thud. "The boss said you wanted to see me but didn't tell me what it was about."

"Thanks for agreeing to speak with us, Mr Davis. I'm DI Sara Ramsey, and this is my partner, DS Carla Jameson."

"Okay, pleased to meet you, I guess. What do you want from me?" He sat back and swept his long fringe to one side as it dropped over his eyes.

"We're investigating two crimes in the area and wondered if you could help us with our enquiries, Tim."

"I'll do my best. You think I might have seen something on my route, is that it?"

"Not really. Okay, please bear with me for now. When was the last time you saw your ex-wife?"

"Sharon?"

"Sorry, do you have more than one?"

"No, I don't. What's going on? Has something happened to her?"

Sara stared at him, gauging his reaction. "If you could just answer the question."

"We met up for lunch a few weeks ago. Why?"

"And you do that type of thing regularly?" Sara found the news surprising. She didn't know many ex-couples who still shared a meal after falling out of love with each other. Maybe there was still a spark left between them?

"Yes, off and on. Just because two people get divorced, it doesn't mean they stop caring about each other."

"Fine. The last time you met her, did she mention if there was anything troubling her?"

"Not really. We made a point of never being negative. We're generally both positive people, if you must know."

"May I ask why you got divorced in that case?"

"Things didn't work out. We simply agreed to part ways, but we still maintain a good friendship. Why? Has she said I've done something to her? What's this about? Why are you questioning me like this?"

Sara let out a long sigh. "I'm sorry to have to tell you that Sharon was murdered over the weekend."

"What? No, this isn't happening. It can't be. Sharon…dead. No, murdered! Who? Bloody hell. I can't think straight. No…she can't be gone. Not Sharon."

Sara placed a hand over his. "Can I get you a glass of water?"

"Yes, please. A double brandy would be preferable, though."

Carla stood. "I'll get it."

She left the room and closed the door behind her.

"I'm sorry to break the news to you at work. You understand the need for us to be here, don't you?"

"Not really. Please tell me you don't think I had anything to do with this?" Sweat beaded his furrowed brow.

"No, we're not sure who is responsible yet. We're doing the groundwork, piecing Sharon's life together to see if anyone can give us a hint of what might have happened. The last time you saw her, did she mention any type of problems in her personal life at all?"

"No, like I said, we always tried to remain positive during our meetings."

"Did she ever reveal what her marriage was like? Or was the subject taboo?"

"She said she'd made the right choice in Martin; they were happy together. In turn, that made me happy. I only ever wanted the best for her. She was a wonderful person who deserved the very best in life."

"Did Martin ever mind you two meeting up?"

"No, he was happy about it, at least, he always said he didn't mind. Has he told you something different? I'm presuming he knows."

"He does. No, he hasn't said anything different to that. And Sharon was happy with Martin, are you sure?"

"Yes, I'm sure. Why? Do you think he had something to do with her murder?"

"No. I have to ask the question. What about work? Was she happy in her role with the Social Services?"

"Happy? I'm not sure she was ever truly happy doing that job. It's not the type of job people go to if they want to have fun during the day, if you get my drift? She saw it more as a calling, really. You know, like joining the priesthood or becoming a nurse or doctor. None of those truly appealed to her, so she opted to try and help people by becoming a social worker. Plus, the fact that she loved kids and wanted to help them in their hour of need."

"Did her caseload ever affect her?"

His gaze dropped to the table, and he swallowed. "If anything, it proved to be the downfall of our marriage. She cared too much and refused to set her job aside when she got home. I loved that girl so much, however, her commitment to her career, well, I couldn't handle it."

"I'm sorry to hear that. So, she was intensely passionate about her career and the people she dealt with?"

"Yes, the more hopeless the case, the more she seemed to want to become involved. It broke both our hearts when we decided to part. Our marriage was stuck in the doldrums. Even when she was supposed to be on holiday, she brought files home to go through. Files she told me she didn't have the time to really focus on at work, due to the stress of the targets she had to meet. I flipped, couldn't hack it any more. I don't think I was expecting too much of her by wanting her to devote some time to me and our marriage. She thought I was being unreasonable and it was she who suggested we get divorced."

"And that didn't go down too well with you, I'm guessing?"

"To begin with, no. She's the only woman I've truly loved. I've shared my life with other women, lived with a few over the years, but no one matched Sharon. I agreed to the divorce on the proviso that we remained in touch."

Carla slipped back into the room and mouthed an apology for interrupting the flow of the conversation. She put the glass of water on the table in front of Tim.

"Thanks," he mumbled and took a gulp.

"You were saying?" Sara probed.

"That's it. We stayed friends, and Martin didn't mind."

"Even though you still loved her?"

His head shot up, and their gazes met. "I *cared about her*, there's a difference between loving and caring for someone, in case you don't know."

"I'm sorry, it was inconsiderate of me to suggest otherwise. Did you ever go to the house? To meet up with Martin, or would that have been too awkward?"

"Once or twice. We all got on well together. I don't understand what you're trying to insinuate here."

"I'm merely trying to grasp what sort of relationships Sharon had with her former husband and her current one, that's all."

"Martin loved her, and she loved him. I think they were better suited than we were. They do the same job, therefore, they can discuss work over dinner or in the evenings. I was out of my depth when she spoke about her job. I'm a bus driver, it's mundane. Most people tend to switch off when I start complaining about the damn traffic in Hereford."

Sara smiled. "It's horrendous most of the time, I have to agree with you."

"She hated me discussing my job when all she was concerned about was trying to care for others. I could see where she was coming from once we had parted, although at the time, I thought she was just being selfish. I can't believe she's gone. You said you're dealing with a couple of cases. Are you saying they're connected in some way?"

"We believe so, however, it's too early to tell yet."

"I'm sorry I can't help you more. I want to. Bloody hell, given the choice I'd willingly go out there and help you hunt down the person who has robbed this world of an angel. She truly was, you know. I know you probably hear a lot of people say that about a victim, but it happens to be true in her case. Martin must be mortified unless…you don't suppose he did it, do you?"

"Why would you even think that, Tim?"

"Ignore me. Grasping at anything and everything that might help you, I suppose. Christ, her parents are going to be beside themselves. Have you told them?"

"No. Her next of kin was her husband. We've had to get on with the investigation and leave him to inform the rest of her family."

"And yet you came here to tell me. No, that's not true, is it? You're questioning me, aren't you? I know you denied it earlier, but I'm getting the distinct impression you believe I have something to do with her death."

"Not at all. I wouldn't be doing my job properly if I didn't ask her former spouse in-depth questions, would I?"

"I suppose not. You're wrong if you think I know anything, just saying. We were more like brother and sister come the end. She brought joy to my life without the sex side of things, if you get what I mean."

"I do. I'm sorry you've lost a dear friend. Please, I'm not accusing you of anything, all I'm trying to do is ascertain if there was anyone in her life who could have possibly held a grudge against her."

"Lots, I'm thinking. Mostly to do with her job. Have you been there?"

"Yes, we've got a few cases to look over. Is there anything that stands out to you which Sharon found upsetting in the past few months?"

He fell silent and stared at the corner of the room, thinking. Eventually, he clicked his fingers. "Okay, this might be a long shot. I remember her being concerned about a case at the end of last year. Something to do with a father who couldn't get in touch with his son because his former partner kept moving to different parts of the UK and she refused to…what did she refuse to do? Shit! I can't for the life of me tell you. You'll need to get in touch with her boss, I think."

"Thanks, we'll do that. Anything else you can think of that you feel might lead us in the right direction?"

"I can't think of anything, no, I'm sorry."

Sara thought he seemed genuinely apologetic, too. "It was worth a try. Sorry to have to break the news to you at work."

"It was a bummer to hear, I can't deny that. I'd rather have heard it from you than in the press or on the news. I'll get in touch with Martin in a day or two, once he's got used to things, to see if I can help him make the funeral arrangements."

"I'm sure Sharon would have appreciated that, if you were as close as you say you were."

The three of them left the room together but went their separate ways at the door. Carla and Sara drove back to the station to see what the team had been up to in their absence.

Sara asked Carla to ring Sandra Duck, to see if the case that Tim had brought up rang any bells with her. She then moved around the room to check what the rest of the team could add to the investigation. Marissa was first up.

"Anything useful, Marissa?"

"Nothing in her past, except she was married for five years to Tim Davis."

"Carla and I have just come from seeing him. I'm not getting the idea he's hiding anything from us. We'll stick his name on the board, just in case."

"She had a brother who died a mysterious death a few years ago. I haven't had a chance to find out anything more about that yet. I was about to see if I could find a PM report on the system."

"Do that as a matter of urgency and let me know the outcome." She moved around the room to Barry. "How's it going, big man?"

"I think I've discovered something fishy, boss. I'm in the process of running it from different angles at present, thought I'd do that before I hunted you down."

"Let me see what you've got." She positioned herself beside him, and he played the footage.

"There's no CCTV outside her work's building, which is bloody annoying considering it's a government one. Anyway, that aside, I caught up with Sharon around the time her shift ended, going through town."

"Oh look, there's a surprise, she's ground to a halt in the traffic. Don't mind me, sounding off as usual, carry on."

He sniggered. "I searched the cars behind her through a few of the cameras located in the town centre, and something stuck out like a sore thumb. This car here. A red Ford Focus. At the start it was a few cars behind. The cars in between drifted off into other lanes at the large roundabout outside Tesco, then the Focus was right behind her here. Tracking them through town, I caught up with them heading in the same direction, however, the car must have dropped back, because now there are a few cars in between them again."

"That's odd, isn't it? You think he was deliberately holding back so that she wouldn't notice him in her mirrors, yes?"

"That's my thinking. I know if I'm in a queue of traffic, I definitely wouldn't be open to letting other cars barge in front of me."

"I'm with you on that one. I tend to put my foot down if someone tries to change lanes. I'm not the giving sort, not where traffic is concerned."

Barry laughed. "I have to say I'm the same. So, here he is again as they head out of town, still holding back, a few cars behind."

"Can we get a plate number?"

"I haven't had a clear enough view of it so far. I'm going to keep trying the different cameras, see what they throw up."

"See if you can get a close-up of the driver while you're at it."

"Leave it with me. I'll give you a shout when I've finished assessing it all."

"Good man. As of now, it's all we have."

Barry nodded, and she walked away.

"Carla, did you chase up forensics about the car?"

"Damn, I forgot. I'm on it now."

Sara bought coffees for the team and distributed them. She lingered by Carla's desk, awaiting an answer.

She hung up and shrugged. "Nothing at all."

"Great. Not what I wanted to hear. I'll bring the board up to date. Barry's spotted a red Ford Focus following Sharon home—at least we're presuming it did. He's still looking into that angle for me."

"Where does that leave us?"

She glanced over at the board. "With two dead women on our hands and no real clues to bloody go on. I'm pondering whether to do a press conference. What do you think?"

Carla's head wobbled from side to side. "Might be worth a shot. What will you tell the public?"

"Exactly! That's my dilemma. I usually like to impart some kind of information in order to get a return from the people on the streets, but this time, I don't really have anything useful to give them."

"Then don't do it."

"But on the other hand, giving one might bring forward an important lead for us to follow up on."

"You're between the Devil and the deep blue sea, aren't you? I don't envy you."

"Thanks. I might run it past the chief, see what she thinks."

Sara took off up the hallway to DCI Price's office. She waited in the outer office with Mary as the chief was in a meeting due to finish any second. She didn't anticipate Superintendent Wagner coming out of the office.

"Ah, DI Ramsey, were your ears burning?"

Sara's cheeks warmed under his scrutinising gaze. She smiled tautly. "No, sir. Should they have been?"

"I'll leave DCI Price to fill you in. I have a full diary today, must dash." With that, he breezed out of the room.

"Shit! Talk about leaving a girl high and dry," she mumbled to Mary.

"He was probably winding you up. Go through, she's aware you're here."

"Thanks." Sara knocked on the door.

"Come in."

Sara stuck her head into the room as if shielding herself against any onslaught on the cards.

"Is it safe?"

Carol frowned. "You tell me. Get in here and stop playing the fool. Whatever is wrong with you?"

"I'd rather keep my distance if you're going to shout at me."

Price expelled a large breath and sat back in her chair. "What do you want?"

"Umm…should you go first? If I'm going to be pulled over the coals, I'd rather get that out of the way, if you don't mind."

"You're wittering on again. What are you going on about?"

"The super asked me if my ears were burning."

"Ah…I'm with you now. Well, that'll teach you to jump to the wrong conclusion. I thought you were better than that, Sara."

"Meaning?"

"Meaning, that the super was in here singling you out for a pat on the back. All right, maybe he tore me off a strip or two in the process, but you came out of it glistening like the bloody Dog Star in the night sky."

"Waxing lyrical isn't really making things any clearer for me, boss."

"Sit down and I'll run through what he said. I'll swerve the part where he slated me."

"I'm still not with you."

"The Laura Tyler case."

"Ouch. He had a pop at you for asking me to take on the case?"

"Yep, issued me with a warning, if you must know."

"Fuck. That's a bit OTT, isn't it?"

"Yep, I thought so. I told him I would resign if he came down heavily on you."

"Whoa! Seriously? You shouldn't have done that, guv. I've got broad shoulders."

"He was gunning for you and would have wiped the floor with you if I hadn't stepped in. Still, the outcome was a good one in the end. I sung your praises as I always do, and he seemed to calm down and take what I was saying on board. Enough about that. What can I do for you?"

"If you're sure you don't mind the extra burden?"

"Are you kidding? I'd welcome the distraction, if I'm honest. Shoot!"

"I'm in a dilemma..." She ran through what they'd managed to obtain on the two current cases so far and asked her advice about whether she should call a press conference or not.

"Hmm...while I completely understand the quandary you find yourself immersed in, I'd go with your gut on this one. What do you hope to achieve?"

"The usual. We need to out this bastard before he ups his game and swoops to pick up another victim."

"There, what did you need to run it past me for then? I trust you, Sara, you're a terrific copper. I've never stood in your way. Every case you've solved under my leadership has turned out to be super success-ful. That's why I trusted you with the Laura case. I realised I'd get into bother for it eventually but I was determined the onus would remain with me and not land on your delicate shoulders. Go, do what you think is necessary to capture this bastard."

"That's quite a speech, boss. I appreciate you having my back as usual. I hope the super sees the error of his ways soon and it doesn't turn into a vendetta against you."

"Thanks. He's wounded at present because I went behind his back and showed some initiative. He'll calm down eventually, I'm sure."

"I hope you're right. I haven't got enough time to manipulate another DCI into my way of thinking."

Carol grinned and sat forward. "I think you've said enough for one day. Watch the door doesn't slap you in the arse on the way out, Inspector."

Sara smiled and left the room. She put things into action with the press officer, Jane, as soon as she returned to the incident room. While she was in her office awaiting the go-ahead from Jane to come through, her phone rang.

"Hello. DI Ramsey. How can I help?"

"I thought I'd ring you as you haven't bothered to get in touch for a few weeks."

Sara closed her eyes, and she leaned her head back as soon as she heard Charlotte, her ex-mother-in-law's voice. "Hi, Charlotte. Forgive me, work has kept me really busy lately. I'm on the hunt for a kil—"

"Don't give me that, Sara. I thought you cared about us. Maybe I was mistaken about that. I treated you like a daughter when Phillip married you. What I didn't anticipate was you discarding us the minute he was laid to rest."

*Shit! It's the same old mantra she keeps spurting. None of which happens to be true!* "I'm sorry if you believe that, Charlotte. Nothing could be further from the truth, I assure you. How's Donald?"

"As if you care?"

"That's harsh, even for you to say. I care, but I'm also a very busy serving police officer, who has been tasked with keeping Hereford safe. It's not as if I have any spare time at the moment, Charlotte. I'm in the throes of tracking down a possible serial killer. I haven't even contacted my own parents for weeks." She bit down on her tongue for telling lies. It was what this woman invariably drove her to do. She had no right dictating what she did and how she spent her time off. Sara made a conscious effort not to say anything about her weekend away with Mark and what that had entailed. The poor woman would probably have another one of her serious meltdowns, like she'd had at the hospital a month or so back when she'd spotted Sara's engagement ring.

A staggered breath filled her ear. "I'm sorry. Please forgive me, Sara. I'm overwrought and anxious about Donald's progress, and lashing out at you was not what I had intended at all."

"Glad to hear it. To say I don't care is so far off the mark. I needn't have visited Donald as much as I have over the past month. I'm glad he's at home now, recuperating. Things will take time for him to get back to normal. Surely the doctors have made you aware of that, haven't they?"

"Yes, you're right. I suppose I'm struggling with caring for our son. Everything is falling on me, and it's hard, much harder, than either Jonathon or I anticipated. He should have stayed in hospital, they would have cared for him so much better than we can here. I'm not a nurse, never have been and never will be."

"If you're not coping then you need to seek help from the authorities, Charlotte. Please, don't take your foul mood out on me when I'm under pressure to get a possible serial killer off the streets." *There, I've said it!* Except, after she'd let rip Sara wished she'd kept her thoughts to herself.

"Well, I never expected to be spoken to like that by you. I thought you had some compassion running through your veins. I'm sorry I rang you now, Sara. You won't be hearing from me again in the future. I think we all need to move on with our lives. You've made it perfectly clear that's your intention by agreeing to marry that man."

"There's no need to be nasty, Charlotte. I'm sorry if I upset you. I'm under as much pressure here as you are there."

"I doubt that very much. Goodbye."

Sara slammed the phone back into its docking station and held her head in her hands for a few minutes, going over the vitriolic attack from Charlotte.

Thankfully, she didn't have to dwell on things for too long as Jane called her.

"Hi, Inspector. We're clear to go at four, is that okay with you?"

"That's superb news. Just what I needed to hear. Thanks for being a saviour once again, Jane."

"My pleasure. I'll see you then."

*F*or Sara, the afternoon dragged by. Charlotte's vicious words constantly circulated her mind like a tornado while she threw herself into the paperwork mounting on her desk. Carla dropped by to give her regular updates on the team's progress, which amounted to very little, along with keeping her caffeine levels topped up.

At five minutes to four, she went downstairs and met up with Jane in the press conference room. She had with her a CCTV image of the red Ford Focus that was of particular interest to the case.

The conference began and soon escalated into a free-for-all for the journalists asking their often inane questions.

"Why are we dealing with yet another murderer walking amongst us, Inspector?" Tory Knight was the first to ask.

"If I knew that, Tory, it would unlock the investigation. Someone out there must recognise this car. You can help us track this person down. At present, we're unsure whether they're involved in either of the crimes. We'd like to speak to the owner of the vehicle to eliminate them from our enquiries."

"What other clues are you working with, Inspector?" Bob Martin from the *Herefordshire Times* asked.

"I need to keep a certain amount close to my chest. What I will tell you is, we're working on several leads, and I personally believe it will only be a matter of time before we capture the culprit. Again, this is why I've called the press conference today. We need the public's help in finding this person."

"And what if a family member of the car owner doesn't come forward, what then?"

"Then we throw more effort into the leads we're currently working on. Either way, we also need the public to remain vigilant at all times. The perpetrator is still at large. I'm not saying that to alarm people, just to make them aware. He appears to be targeting younger women. But who's to say if his MO won't alter, if he has an agenda he's working on? Stay safe and vigilant. That concludes the conference. I'd like to thank you all for attending."

Jane and Sara moved through the murmuring crowd and left the room together.

"Thanks, Jane. Fingers crossed it's done the trick."

"Mine will be tightly crossed for you. See you soon."

"Not too soon, I hope." She raced back up the stairs.

The team had been watching the live streaming on the TV and were making their way back to their seats when she entered the room.

"You did really well, given the information you had to go on," Carla told her.

"It's still frustrating the hell out of me. Okay, I'm going to need someone to volunteer to man the phones until say about eleven, who's up for that?"

Craig's hand instantly flew up in the air.

"Thanks, Craig. I'll get a pizza delivered, that should keep you going for a while."

"There's no need for you to do that, boss. I'm happy to work the extra hours without recompense if it means finding this bastard sooner."

And that was why she loved working with this team so much, their commitment was legendary. Second to none. "I'll still buy you one. What sort? I'll get it ordered now, for what, eight o'clock?"

"If you insist. I know I'm going to take some flak for my choice, but I'll have a Hawaiian, and yes, I love pineapple on my pizza. It reminds me of a holiday in Florida I had last year."

Sara chuckled. "Okay, each to their own." She marched into the office and looked up the local pizza parlour's number on her mobile and placed the order.

Two hours later, she and the rest of the team, all except Craig, said farewell and left for the evening. It had been a long day, and she was in dire need of a cuddle. She rang Mark's mobile.

"Hi, I was thinking about you."

"You were? Smutty thoughts?"

"Hardly. I was wondering what to do for dinner."

"You disappoint me, oh, fiancé of mine. I'm on my way home now. What time will you be finished tonight?"

"I've got an emergency on the way in. I doubt I'll be home before eight or nine, hence me thinking about you. I was on the verge of calling you to tell you I'd be delayed."

"What's for dinner, do we know?"

"There's some lasagne left over from last week in the freezer, you could defrost that."

"I don't fancy it. I'll stop off at the shops, see what I can pick up. See you later, miss you already."

"Miss you, too. Can't wait to be in your arms again."

"You old romantic you."

"Not so much of the old, and damn right I'm a romantic. I love you, Sara."

"Love you, too."

She ended the call, changed direction at the next set of lights and drove back into town, thinking that Morrisons would be her best bet for filling a basket at this time of night.

Once she pulled into the car park and saw the lack of vehicles, she decided to grab a trolley and do a full shop instead.

An hour later, she loaded up her three bags and drove home to the sound of an eighties' CD. Her neighbour, Ted, was passing the house with Muffin the poodle and offered to help carry the bags into the kitchen for her. She declined.

"Get away with you. I'm fine, a little exertion isn't going to harm me. How's Mavis? We need to get together soon, lots to tell you about."

"She's fine. Yes, let's try and make plans for the weekend. I take it your trip to Scotland went better than anticipated by the glint in your eye."

"It did. It's a phenomenal place. We're so looking forward to having it as our venue."

"We used to holiday in Scotland with Susie." His smile departed, and a dark cloud covered his face.

She dropped the two bags she was holding and hugged him. "Think about the memories you shared together. The good times, Ted. It works for me every time Philip springs to mind."

Susie had gone off seeking adventure in the outback and got killed by a local madman. Her death had caused Mavis and Ted unimaginable pain. She supposed that was why they were so close now. Although they'd only known each other a couple of years, since moving in to the new estate within weeks of each other, it was their sadness at losing a loved one that had probably drawn them together. Anyway, Sara believed that speaking openly to each other about Susie's and Philip's murders, had acted as grief counselling sessions for them all, over the past couple of years, without the added trauma of going to a counsellor.

"I do, love. Sometimes it catches me out. You understand where I'm coming from, I know you do."

"Only too well. You know I'm always here for you. Do you want to come in for a chat and a cuppa now? You'd be more than welcome to."

"No. I'll give that a miss, lovely. You've got enough on your plate as it is. I'd better get back to Mavis or she'll think I've run off with the old girl round the corner who's had her eye on me since we moved in."

"As if. Blimey, don't say that. She'd kill you if you sank to those levels, and quite frankly, well, I've had my share of dealing with murder cases to last me a lifetime."

Gently, he laid a hand on her cheek. "You're an amazing person, Sara. So glad to have you in our lives."

"Ditto. Now shoo! See you over the weekend. We'll firm up plans for dinner soon. It's our turn to cook, I believe."

"No hassle from us, love. Only if you can spare the time."

"Always, for you two, Ted. Have a good evening."

"You, too. Will Mark be home soon?"

"I'm hoping so. Another emergency op which always seems to take place in the evening. If I was one of those women with a suspicious mind, I might think he was having an affair on the side. Luckily, I'm not. Oh dear, what am I saying? I'm a copper, of course I have the obligatory suspicious mind."

They both laughed. She unlocked the front door, ferried the two bags in, and then returned for the third bag. When she returned to shut the front door, Misty had joined her in the hallway and was rubbing herself up against one of the carriers.

She bent down and picked her up. "Hello, you. Did you miss me?"

Misty's unmistakable joy at seeing her was reflected in the loud purring filling the hallway.

She carried Misty into the kitchen along with one of the bags then returned for the other two. Sara glanced up at the clock on the wall, shocked to see it was already seven o'clock. She put Misty down on the floor and hurriedly set about unpacking the shopping and flinging it in the cupboards. She left out the ingredients she'd sourced for tonight's dinner and got to work on the preparations. In between, she fed Misty and put her out in the garden.

Mark came home at five minutes to eight. He'd called ahead to say he was on his way. Dinner was ready to be dished up as he walked through the front door. He snuggled into her neck and wrapped his arms around her waist. "That smells wonderful. I'll have to be late more often if this is the result."

She swivelled in his arms and playfully punched his chest. "Oh no you don't, buster. I'm stressed to the bloody hilt, throwing all this together. I don't mind doing it at the weekend, but during the week is a bit too much."

He chuckled. "Why do it then? I don't expect it from you."

"I know. I wanted to do something nice for you. Ugh…don't listen to me. Pour the wine, would you? No, wait…" She sniffed the air. "You need a shower first."

"Nothing like a subtle hint to put me in my place, and no, that wasn't very subtle of you. I'll be down in five, dish up, I'll be good."

He bounced out of the room, and she tested the broccoli spears a final time with a sharp knife.

"Right, another two minutes and everything should be ready. That'll give Mark enough time to jump in the shower."

After laying the table, she removed the dishes she had warming in the oven and plated up. Mark came back into the room, his hair damp, wearing a clean T-shirt and jeans.

Her heart joined her stomach doing a combined somersault. "Ready?"

"I'm starving. Drink?"

"There's a bottle chilling in the freezer, it should be cold enough by now."

They ate their meal, which consisted of salmon, broccoli and carrots, accompanied by a chickpea mash, which she'd never served up before, and it all went down a treat.

Mark insisted he should be the one to clear up. She didn't argue as she was dead on her feet by now. Sara picked up Misty again and settled on the couch. She laid her head back and closed her eyes. The next thing she knew, Mark's lips gently brushed hers.

"Tough day, huh? Do you need to talk about it or do you want to avoid the subject altogether?"

"One of those days when you seem to take two steps forward and ten steps back. We think we've got something significant, only to find our hopes dashed. How was your day? By the smell of you, I'd say eventful."

Mark sniggered. "You could say that. I've grappled with a python, been shat on by a parrot. A dog cocked his leg up my trousers the second I gave him his yearly jab. There's something else, but I think that was more than enough to contend with."

"Ah, the glamorous side of being a Supervet."

"Hardly, I'll take being known as a good vet, there's nothing super about what I do."

"I disagree. I think you're amazing. You saved my pussy, remember?"

He laughed. "There's an answer to that, but I'm too much of a gent to go there."

The rest of the evening consisted of them going over the final plans for the wedding and having a cuddle, all three of them.

Reluctantly, Sara called time on her day. Her sagging eyelids told her if she didn't get to bed soon, she'd end up falling asleep in situ on the couch.

## 10

He sat in his van, watching, waiting for his next victim to appear. His hands slipped on the steering wheel, sweat slicking his palms. This wasn't him, not really. He was a genuinely nice guy. These people had turned him into what he'd become. He swallowed down the bile that had surfaced and burned his throat on the way up. He'd formed a new persona now, it was the only way he could cope with the danger. Danger he'd created—no, that was wrong. *They* were to blame. They'd pushed him to the extreme, and now he was caught up in it, fully invested in the plan. It was far too late for him to back out. He had regrets, of course he did. But there was also an underlying sense of empowerment accompanied by satisfaction to his actions, too.

Those without sin…

These people were the sinners, not him. He was serving the community, he truly believed that. Getting rid of the people who put others in danger, despite what they believed. Helpfulness was overrated. A cheap word that meant nothing. Was it helpful to break up a loving family? Helpful to whom? Not the family, that was for sure. Do-gooders were okay most of the time, except when they stuck their nose in and messed up. Not once, not even twice, numerous times. One letter had started the ball rolling. Everything had escalated dramatically, and quickly, after that.

All he wanted now was what was rightfully his. His child needed the stability he could offer and was prepared to give him. The idea of that coming to fruition was so far off the mark, why? Because of *these* people. They'd done their best to work together, to plan his downfall. They opened their ears and listened to *her,* condemning him for things he'd never done.

Hard truths can be dealt with, triumphed over, but lies will destroy the soul… He'd read that somewhere recently, and it held more than a note of accuracy for him.

His heart thundered. His gaze glued on the woman as she left the building. His hand automatically reached for the key in the ignition and turned it. The woman said a cheerful goodbye to someone and went to the far corner of the car park. Now was the time to make his move. The van jolted forward once he put his foot on the accelerator. She glanced his way and pressed the key fob to open the driver's door to her BMW. He halted abruptly beside her and jumped out.

"What's the meaning of this? How dare you come here and behave in this manner…?"

"Shut the fuck up and get in the van."

"I will *not.* Get out of my way or I'll call the police."

His temper frayed as soon as she mentioned the police. His fist connected with her face. She went down, her legs crumpling beneath her, and she hit her head on the car door on the way down.

"Hey, what's going on over there?" a woman in her forties or fifties shouted. She had her phone out and was punching in a number.

*Quick, do something. Think fast!* He dragged the woman's heavy frame into the back of the van. She was out cold, a blessing. He'd much rather deal with a limp body than someone putting up a fight.

"Hey, you. Stop right there. I've called the police. They're on their way. Don't do this. Leave Miss Vickers alone."

He scrambled behind the steering wheel, slammed the van into reverse and drove towards the exit. The mouthy woman stood in his path. She was either brave or stupid, he couldn't tell which. Her determined stance pissed him off. He squeezed his foot down on the accelerator, and he aimed at her.

She remained in the same position and raised her hand. "Stop! I won't let you pass!"

"Get out of the way you, stupid bitch," he shouted out the open window.

It was too late. Her determination won out in her refusal to move. He struck her at speed. Sent her reeling as the van clipped her. He watched in the rear-view mirror; her body rolled a few times across the tarmac and then came to an abrupt stop. He rebuffed the idea of making sure she was okay and continued to drive, keeping a watchful eye on his speed. The last thing he needed was to attract the attention of the police with Vickers unconscious in the back.

He drove out to the warehouse and yanked her out of the van. He had her tied up, ready for a dunking before she regained consciousness.

Now all he had to do was wait until she woke up. He had all the time in the world for that. The thought of nipping out to buy fish and chips even crossed his mind. "That can wait. It'll be my treat when all this is over."

He sat on a lump of concrete beside the woman. He was in no rush to get this over. Not today.

Approximately an hour later, the woman stirred. "Please, what are you doing? Why are you doing this?"

He pushed himself to his feet. "Why do you guys always persist in asking dumb questions? You know me, right?"

She narrowed her eyes and peered at him. "No, I don't think so. Who are you? Why have you kidnapped me?"

"That's simple, because I can. There was no one there to stop me. Oh, that woman tried, but I dealt with her."

"Which woman? What did you do?"

"Probably killed her. She deserved it. Nosey bloody parker, sticking her beak into something that doesn't concern her. Oh wait, that could, and should, be directed at you as well."

"I think you've made a genuine mistake. I don't know you or what you're going on about."

"You want me to enlighten you? Fill you in on all the gory details?"

"Yes, please. I'd love things to be clearer. I'm struggling to comprehend what's going on here."

"It's not difficult for a woman in your position, and I don't mean at this particular time, to comprehend what goes on in people's lives. You have a moral responsibility to ensure children are safe after all. You failed my little boy, not once, not twice, but numerous times."

"I did? I'm unaware of any such failings. Let me go, and I'll do anything you want me to do to make things right for you. You're clearly upset about something major that has happened in your life. We can work through this together, if you'll give me a chance."

He tipped his head back and laughed. "Give you a chance? You and that other bitch you worked with, Linda Strong, had numerous chances to put things right. You blocked out all sentiment. Anything I told you was disregarded with a click of your fingers. I'm not the only father you've let down over the years either. Did you know there was a Facebook group about your school? Set up by other fathers in my position. Fathers you've regrettably failed over the years. Fathers wanting to be with their children who have been blocked by your school from having any contact with them. Have you any idea what that's doing to the children? The mental abuse these kids sustain during a break-up from the mothers who refuse to let their children have anything to do with their fathers? Not every father is bad, you know. Sometimes, there are those who only want the best for their child, but the system lets them down."

"I'm just part of the system. A cog, if you like. If you give me your details, I'll see what I can do to rectify things. All is not lost, you must never think that."

"Oh, but it is. She's made sure of that. Cut me out of his life, and all of you have ensured she gets away with it. At what cost? At the cost of my sanity, that's what. To you, all of you, you're dealing with a family on paper, you forget those names have lives, precious lives that often can't survive without other family members who they've been cut off from."

"I'm sorry. I'm hearing you now. If it's not too late, I'd like to help you."

He hesitated. Paused his thoughts to mull over what she'd said, however, his anger intensified. He'd heard all the platitudes before, over the past two years, but he was no further forward, and now it was time to punish those who'd seriously let him down, along with all the other fathers out there in the same position. This was for them as well.

"It's far too late for that. This is my time. The time has come for me to obtain retribution for my lad. You're guilty of mentally torturing my son. When I was in contact with him, he told me he used to ask you and Strong if he could ring his daddy from school. You denied him that opportunity."

"We had to. The mother has rights."

He struck her face. "Every father has a right to be with his child, you forget that."

"Not every father is as considerate as you, I can assure you."

"Don't you think I know that? The money I've spent over the past year or so should have told you what sort of man I am. The type who can't live without his son in his life. But you lot couldn't give a fucking shit, could you? Do you have kids?"

"Yes, they're older, fifteen and sixteen."

"And how do you think they would feel if someone cut you out of their lives?"

"I dread to think. It wouldn't happen, I'd make sure of that."

He glared at her. "See, now you're getting it. I've been stuck in a tornado of emotions for two years now. All I've ever tried to do is the right thing for my son, and you lot dug your heels in, prevented me from doing that. Not every mother cares for her son correctly. You think it's right to keep a child up until eight o'clock every night so the father can feed him when he comes home from work? Despite the mother being at home all day?"

"No, I'll admit, that's wrong."

"Or for that child to be treated no better than a dog and kept in a cage, along with the dog?"

"I had no idea. I'm sorry."

"I told you. You have a selective memory. The days I came home from work and that child was sitting in a wet or soiled nappy is nobody's business. How can that be what's right for the child? I'm nothing without my son. I love every part of that child with my heart and my soul. I would never, I have never, laid a hand on him in my life. He only ever recognised love from me, and now…now, I can't even speak to the child. I have a court order giving me access to him, and *she* won't allow it. The court don't give a damn either. What's the use of having a court order in place? It's a legally binding document, but here I find myself, beating the same old drum. No one gives a shit about what happens to others, as long as it doesn't involve them."

"I'm sorry. If you release me, I'll do everything I can to put things right for you. I won't even go to the police. I promise to help you. See to it that your child is returned to you."

"It's too late. Your futile words are worthless now. You're only saying these things because of the mortal situation you find yourself in. Your kids will soon understand what it's like to never see their mother again. At least they're older, they'll be able to process things better. How do you think a five-year-old copes without seeing his father on a regular basis? The one person in his life who fed and clothed him properly? I spoke to him a few months ago. She'd just fed him; he ate his dinner in front of me. What do you suppose that meal consisted of?"

"I'm sorry, I can't even hazard a guess. Something disgusting?"

"He was eating a tin of spaghetti hoops from the can. A cold meal on a freezing winter's day, and you all believed the lies she told you over me. I fear for my boy's health, and yet, no one is willing to listen to me. I understand you probably think it's sour grapes, I get that. Your perception is wrong, though. Why doesn't someone take the time to sit that boy down and ask him? Does he not count in all this? Apparently not. He's as skinny as a child from Auschwitz, and yet, you all sit back in your comfortable chairs in your expansive offices and don't give a flying fuck. I'm at my wits' end. But I'll tell you this…killing the other two righted some of the injustice you guys are guilty of doing against me and my son. The truth is, I want more…"

He winched the seat up and swung it over the barrel. She screamed and thrashed around as he lowered her into the cold water. This time he had no intention of toying with her. He was tired, fed up and missing his son terribly.

One of Kenzie's toys called to him. He blocked out the noise behind him and walked a few paces to pick up the miniature yellow JCB. Tears blurred his vision. Thoughts of playing with his son, holding him tightly so not a soul could hurt him ever again, crowded his mind. The tears trickled onto his cheeks, and his heart ached for the son he was unable to touch, to hold, to hug, to love. The one guy in this world he cherished more than life itself, who was so far out of his grasp. Why? Because of people like Heidi Vickers and the others who were now on their way to meeting their maker.

He returned to the barrel. The silence gratified him. Gave him a sense of closure for one part of his life at least. But it didn't dull the restless ache in his heart. He hadn't had any contact with Kenzie for months now, that was what all this was truly about. For all he knew… Kenzie could be dead. Therefore, those who had let his son down deserved to die as well.

He winched the headmistress' body out and swung the seat off to the right. He'd let the excess water seep away for the next few hours and then dispose of the body. His workload had increased tenfold in the last week, but it had all been worth it.

# 11

———

"Sorry to trouble you, ma'am."

Sara sat forward in her chair. Judging by the desk sergeant's tone, he was troubled by something he felt was important. "Go on, Jeff."

"We've got reports of one woman possibly being abducted and another who was mown down by the vehicle when she tried to prevent the driver leaving the scene."

"My God. Where?"

"This is what made me get in touch with you. I wouldn't ordinarily, you know that."

"I know. Where?"

"Lossworth Primary."

"Shit! Do we know who was abducted?"

"The person who placed the call said it looked like the headmistress. When they got closer to where it happened, they realised the headmistress' car was still in the car park."

In a fit of anger, she threw the pen she was holding across her desk. "Shit, damn and blast! And the woman who was mown down?"

"She's in hospital. The ambulance arrived and managed to resuscitate her. If they hadn't shown up, she would have died, according to the witness."

"Fuck. Who is the witness?"

"A Lance Murray. I've got his number and address, figured you'd want to speak with him."

"Brilliant. Give me the details, Jeff. I'll get my guys working on things at this end ASAP."

"Thought you might." He read out the information, and Sara jotted it down.

She shot out of her chair and called for everyone's attention. "Listen up, guys. A major incident has occurred. An abduction and a possible attempted murder took place at Lossworth Primary. The headmistress was the one taken. Shit. Carla, you and I need to get over there, work the scene. Craig, you and Will come with us. We're going to need to try and find more witnesses before the trail goes cold. It's probably too late...no, I mustn't think that way. According to the witness who called it in, another woman is in hospital. The paramedics saved her life at the scene."

"Jesus. It has to be the same perp, doesn't it? Why? Will the rest of the staff be at risk now? Should we advise them to shut the school down for the next few days?" Christine said.

"Good call. We have to. Whether they'll be willing to take our advice on board is another matter entirely. Christine, do your best to make that happen while we're out, will you?"

"I'll get on it right away, boss."

"Come on, gang. Let's go."

The four of them raced down the stairs and piled into two cars. Sara led the charge to the scene, adrenaline kicking in and driving her actions.

"Why the headmistress of the school?" Carla mumbled.

"It has to be something to do with a child attending that school. That's the angle we need to be working on."

"In connection with Social Services, I'm guessing, right?"

"Yep. Thinking over the files Sandra Duck let us take a look at, is anything ringing a bell with you? Did any of the children those files referred to go to Lossworth?"

Carla shook her head. "I don't recall that school being mentioned, do you?"

"No. Which leads me to think all the information we gathered at the Social Services is shite and not relevant to the investigation. Bollocks, just when we thought there was a chink of light at the end of this long tunnel."

"Don't be such a defeatist. I'll get Marissa to ring Sandra Duck, ask her to sift through Sharon Ryman's casefiles to see if she can find any connections leading back to the primary school."

"Well done. Ensure they're both aware how urgent this is now. The killer has an exact agenda by the look of things and isn't willing to deviate from it, I'm guessing. We need to find out who he is and stop him in his tracks."

"I know, preferably before another body ends up on the slab, right?"

"You've got it, partner. Get dialling."

By the time Sara arrived at the school, Carla had ended her call and got Marissa on the case.

"We need to get these people cleared," Sara growled. "Can you see to that? Or get one of the boys to get these people out of here. Where are uniform? They should've cordoned off the area. What is wrong with people?"

"Calm down. I'll ring Jeff, tell him to get a few men down here now."

Sara flung her door open and approached Craig and Will. "We need to search this crowd for witnesses and then send the others home. Carla is calling for backup. Push them back for now, guys, they're trampling all over the bloody crime scene for fuck's sake."

"Leave it with us."

Will and Craig dashed over to the crowd, their arms spread out, and shepherded the throng of rubberneckers back to the edge of the pavement.

Sara joined Carla, and together they walked the scene, ensuring they remained a few feet away from the car with its door open which, Sara presumed belonged to Vickers.

"Looks like her car was wedged in, maybe the perp's vehicle hit her car door. Either way, we'll get SOCO on it. Here's Will, perhaps he's got something useful for us."

"Guv, I've got another witness. The bloke lives in the house just there. He saw us pull up and wanted to speak to someone straight away. He saw everything, apparently."

"I'll have a word."

Sara and Will made their way back to the man.

"Will you take notes for me, Will?"

He fished his notebook out of his pocket and promptly dropped it on the floor. "Damn!"

Sara shook her head, exasperated, then shrugged off the incident rather than get frustrated.

"This is Mr Boyd. I'll let him fill you in."

"Mind if we step away from the crowd, Mr Boyd? Will is going to take notes, if that's all right?"

"Sure. I'd just come home from work and I was looking for my keys when I heard a squeal of tyres. I turned round to see a guy in a white van bundling a woman into the back. I have to be honest with you, I was crapping myself, didn't know whether to get involved or not. I hate any sort of conflict usually, you see. Anyway, while I was deliberating, this woman called out and tried to stand in the way of the speeding vehicle. Bloody idiot, there was only ever going to be one winner in that situation."

"And yet you weren't the person who rang nine-nine-nine."

"That's right. I told you, I don't like any trouble."

Sara cocked an eyebrow. "And yet there was a woman lying on the ground, fighting for her life."

"Yes, I know that now, I didn't know it at the time, though."

*What the fuck? And that's a logical argument, is it?*

"We'll leave that angle for now. At least someone had the decency to ring for an ambulance without missing a heartbeat. That person probably saved that woman's life."

His head dropped, and he muttered an apology. "Sorry, I should have been more thoughtful and less selfish."

"Your words, not mine. Did you get a good look at the licence number?"

"No. I was too concerned…I mean, I was…no, sorry, I screwed up, didn't I?"

"Somewhat! Never mind, tell my colleague what you can remember about the vehicle." Sara walked away and went in search of Craig to see if he'd had better luck. "Anything useful come to light?"

"Not really. A few people saw the van drive away."

"I don't suppose anyone got the plate number?"

"Nope. When I asked, they seemed a bit confused by the question."

"What the actual…? Jesus, and people are quick to jump on us for not carrying out our job correctly. It's bloody hard without the public pulling their frigging weight. Shit, now I'm sodding angry. I need to calm down. That's SOCO arriving now. I'll have a word with them instead. Keep asking the question, Craig. You never know your luck, there might be a genius lingering in the crowd somewhere."

Craig sniggered.

Mac Rogers was instructing his two colleagues on how to proceed when Sara arrived.

"Hi, Mac, how's it diddling?"

"Things would be going well if we didn't get a call like this nearing the end of our damn shift."

"Them's the breaks, mate. Let me run through what we have here."

"If you must. We'll tog up while you do that, okay?"

"Suits me." She went over everything she knew and pointed out the damage on Vickers' car she needed them to concentrate on. "I've just spoken to a key witness who tells me we're looking for a white van. In the event we catch this bastard, I need you to confirm his vehicle struck the victim's. Or should I say the woman he's abducted. I'm hoping we can get to her before the victim status descends on her. Am I making any bloody sense at all?" She punched her temple with a clenched fist.

"Yeah, you're tying yourself into knots by the sound of it, but I get your drift. Leave it with me. You think this case is connected to the two you're already working on?"

"Yep, we think so. Too much of a coincidence to think otherwise. Do your best to get the results back to me ASAP, if you would."

"You've got my word."

Sara left him to it and caught up with Carla. "People can be so infuriating at times."

Carla frowned. "Mac and his team? What did he say?"

"No, I wasn't talking about him." She motioned towards the guy Will was still talking to. "He didn't want to get involved, saw everything, but he didn't do anything."

"What? He wasn't the one who reported the incident?"

"Nope. Prat. I wish we could sling a charge at him."

"Worth putting him on our radar," Carla grumbled.

"Nah, it wouldn't be worth the hassle. Reinforcements have arrived." Sara pointed at the two squad cars pulling into the car park. Then she glanced around. "No CCTV footage in the area, which is bollocks, no frigging help to us whatsoever."

"Strange for a primary school not to have it in place. We need to see why. Maybe someone in a nearby house will come forward, if they've got a secret camera keeping an eye on what goes on in their garden."

"Is that you living in hope?"

"Maybe. What next?"

"We'll hang around for a few minutes. I'm going to ring the station, get a next of kin. We'll need to stop off and make them aware of the situation and then we can toddle off back to base. I get the sense we're wasting our time being here."

She rang the station and asked Barry to search for the information she needed. After several grunts of disappointment, he finally announced, "I've got it. Karl Vickers, thirty-one Wallace Ave, Burghill."

"Cheers, Barry. We'll nip out there now. There's nothing further we can do here."

She had a word with Will, passed on the witnesses' details for him and Craig to chase up and left the area. Sara sped through the town, on a mission. She noticed Carla's nails digging into the passenger seat.

"Am I driving too fast?"

"Depends if you're Lewis Hamilton or not."

Sara laughed. "Sorry. I'll slow down a bit."

Carla's fingers unfurled, and the rest of the journey consisted of less dangerous swerves around the corners, a slower drive, which was more to her partner's liking.

The Vickers' house was a grand affair. A Georgian type with a spectacular columned porch.

"Sodding hell. We unquestionably see the variance of wealth in this county on our visits, don't we?"

Carla whistled. "Bloody Nora, you could say that. We're definitely in the wrong damn jobs. Do we know what the husband does for a living?"

"No, Barry didn't say. I'm guessing he's someone important, judging by this pad. I can't see a headmistress of a primary school being on much, can you?"

"Nope."

Their heels sank into the deep gravel on the way to the front door. There was a silver Mercedes parked close by. Sara let out a sigh of relief. At least they hadn't had a wasted trip. She pulled on the ornate bell and heard it echo around the house before the front door was answered by a smartly dressed man in his late forties or early fifties.

"Can I help? We don't deal with salesmen on our doorstep."

"Glad to hear it." Sara produced her warrant card. "DI Sara Ramsey, and this is my partner, DS Carla Jameson. Are you Mr Vickers?"

His brow wrinkled. "That's right. Karl Vickers. May I ask what you want?"

"It would be better if we spoke inside, sir." It really made no odds to Sara, not in this instance, as there were no nosey neighbours to overhear their conversation, but she was eager to see inside the house from her own inquisitive perspective.

"Is that necessary? Maybe you could give me a hint of what this is about first."

"Your wife, sir."

He relented and motioned for them to come in. The hallway was dominated by black-and-white tiles and a grand sweeping staircase. On the walls, the couple had kept up the theme of black and white in the numerous paintings and photos that were positioned up the stairs. It was quite breathtaking, really.

"Will here do?"

"Of course. We don't want to intrude, sir."

"Yes, yes. You said this had to do with my wife. I'm expecting her home any moment now. I finished work early as we have tickets for the theatre in Birmingham this evening. We'll be setting off as soon as she's changed, so she won't have time to answer any of your questions. Therefore, I would suggest it would be better if you contacted her at school tomorrow."

Sara chewed on her lip while he spoke. "Ah, well, earlier we were called to her place of work...and, when was the last time you spoke to your wife?"

"A couple of hours ago, around two, if you must know. Why? What aren't you telling me, Inspector?"

"The reason behind our visit today is to inform you that we believe your wife has been abducted."

His head jutted forward, and his eyes widened. "You can't be serious. What makes you think that?"

"We have two witnesses who said they saw a woman, matching your wife's description, being bundled into a van before it sped off."

His hand clawed at his hair. "This is bizarre, too bizarre to take in. Why would anyone want to take Heidi? Do you know who has her?"

"We believe it's part of an ongoing investigation, actually connected to two cases we're working on. I wondered if you wouldn't mind trying to ring your wife's mobile for us, sir. The odds are the person who is holding her has probably switched it off so we can't trace it."

"Of course. Damn, where did I put my phone?" He glanced over at the console table. There was a bunch of car keys on it but nothing else.

Sara and Carla followed him into a stunning kitchen which was probably the size of Sara's entire house. There, lying on the marble kitchen island, was his phone. He snatched it up and punched in his password, then he scrolled through and hit redial. He shook his head. "Nothing. It's not even connected."

"I'm sorry to hear that. It's as I suspected. I have to ask if Heidi has had any kind of threats recently. Anything that's been bothering her?"

"No, not that I can think of. She has a fairly stressful job, we both do."

"And what do you do, sir?"

"I'm a solicitor with Taylor, Johnson and Metcalfe in Hereford."

"I see. So, nothing is coming to mind?"

"Yes, there is something. I'd like to pick up on what you said when you arrived."

"What's that?"

"You said you believe her abduction, kidnapping or whatever spin you want to put on it, was connected to two cases you're already investigating."

Sara nodded. "That's our assumption at this stage."

"Are you suggesting this has something to do with Linda Strong being murdered a few days ago?" His clenched hand clutched the front of his hair, and he rested it against his forehead.

"I'm sorry, I can't lie to you. Yes, I believe there's a connection there."

"And another case? A murder case?"

Sara blew out an exasperated breath. "Yes, I believe so. Which is why we're doing all we can to find your wife, sir. There's an alert out on the vehicle as we speak. I wanted to drop by and inform you in person rather than have you hear about it on the evening news later."

"Thank you. I'm grateful to you for that. Do you know who has her? Who killed Linda?"

"Not yet. We're working tirelessly to find that out."

"The other case, can you tell me who the victim is? Maybe I can help piece things together."

"The second victim is a Sharon Ryman, she's a social worker."

His cheeks puffed out, and he shook his head. "Nope, her name doesn't ring any bells with me at all. Oh God..." He pulled out a stool and flopped onto it. "Please, you have to do something, I don't want to lose Heidi. I can't lose her, she's all I've got. We have so many plans for the future. Early retirement is on the cards, and we're going to go on crazy adventures around the world. We've devoted our lives to work, sacrificed so much, and now...she's missing."

"Please, you have to try and remain positive, Karl. We're doing our best to get her back."

"Are you? What are you doing, apart from putting out an alert?"

"My team are working hard to get your wife back, sir, they're still at the scene, gathering witness statements and all the relevant facts we need to get the investigation started."

"Is that enough? What if...I can't bring myself to consider what might have happened to her by now."

"You have my word that we won't rest until we find her. Please, we need your help. We need something to go on. We have no idea who this person is or why he's going after his targets. Are you sure you can't think of anything that Heidi might have been concerned about lately?"

"No, nothing is coming to mind at all. I fear you're wasting your time being here when you should be out there looking for my wife."

"Okay, we'll leave it there. Here's a card. If you think of anything, will you ring me?"

"Likewise, Inspector."

"That goes without saying, sir."

He accompanied them to the front door. "Please, do all you can to bring her home safely."

"You have my word."

.   .   .

*J*t was six-thirty by the time Sara and Carla joined the others in the incident room.

"Marissa, any news from Sandra Duck?"

"She told me she couldn't delve into anything this evening as she was due at a function for the Samaritans and couldn't get out of it. I asked her to get on it first thing, and she agreed."

"Okay, I was hoping for better news than that. Shit, what does it take for people to go out of their way to cooperate with us? Two women already dead and another abducted as well as one more lying in hospital. That reminds me, I need to ring the hospital to see how that poor woman is."

"It's so damn frustrating, unless…" Carla said and then sipped on a cup of coffee Christine had just handed her.

"Unless? Don't stop there," Sara demanded.

"Unless Sandra Duck is in on this?"

"This? We don't even know what 'this' is yet. You seriously think she could be?"

"What else have we got to go on?"

"She's too nice. I can't see it myself. What are you doing, Christine?" Sara glanced over at the sound of busy fingers tapping away at the keyboard.

"I just thought I might as well start searching her background."

Sara smiled. "Leaping ahead of the obvious order coming your way, eh?"

"That's right. I'll make a start this evening. I'm not in a rush to go home."

"Barry, I need you to source the usual CCTV footage from the streets close to the school."

"I've already requested that, boss. I should have it by the morning." He grimaced.

"Bloody hell! Okay, if that's the best we can do, you guys might as well go home. Christine and I will stay here for a few hours to man the fort. I wouldn't feel right going home, knowing that a woman's life is in mortal danger. There's no point all of us working overtime."

"If you're sure? I'd volunteer to stay, but Gary needs me there with him at night. That's when his aches and pains tend to surface, after he's exerted himself during the day, either at work or during his physio sessions," Carla said, her tone apologetic.

"There's no need to feel bad. Go, before I change my mind."

The rest of the team left the station ten minutes later. Sara picked up the black marker and brought the whiteboard up to date. Her mind wandered, exploring different scenarios and, in the distance, Christine's fingers clacking kept her company.

A few hours later, over a slice of pizza and a coffee, they debated what Christine had discovered.

"It's so infuriating. We've got nothing to go on with this one."

Christine nodded. "I know. I did my best with what was to hand on Sandra, but nothing showed up. She's divorced and remarried. No record to speak of, which is a good thing considering the position she holds."

Sara wiped her greasy fingers on a napkin and then ran it over her lips. "And that's it, I didn't really expect to find anything in her past. She wouldn't be allowed to work for Social Services had something shown up."

"True enough. So, where do we go from here?"

"Not sure, is the brutal and honest answer. We've got uniform on high alert, searching for a white van. Christ, they're in for a bloody busy night, knowing how many vans are on the road in this area. Admittedly, they're more likely to be on the road during the course of the day rather than at night. We're waiting for that one break that usually turns an investigation on its head, and nothing is forthcoming yet. What does that tell us? Apart from us being useless?"

"Don't say that, boss. We're all doing our best. The break will come eventually, it has to. It's a difficult task if the perp is cagey and covering his back the way he is."

"Is he, though? I'm not convinced of that. He's abducting these women in broad daylight, at least in Sharon's and Heidi's cases. Why take the risk? What's going through his mind the minute he abducts them? These women were tortured, why? What's the reasoning behind that? Why do people usually torture others?"

"To obtain information from them."

"Yeah, the question is, what information? Carla and I discussed this earlier; it has to relate to a child's case. Anyway, there's no point beating ourselves up about things, we've done our bit tonight. Let's go home and start afresh tomorrow. Maybe Sandra will make our day by giving us a name we can latch on to. As things stand, we've got bugger all going for us."

"One last thing I think we should consider."

Sara rested her elbows on her knees. "What's that?"

"What if there's more than one perp?"

Sara stretched her neck. It clicked as she twisted it from side to side. "Throwing that into the mix is only going to heap more pressure on us. You're talking about the different vehicles used, right?"

"Yep. Three different ones so far."

"You could have something there, unless the perp has access to more than one vehicle—that could very well be a possibility."

"It could be."

"Good thinking. First thing in the morning, we'll run that past the others and, between us, come up with possible outlets to try. See, doing overtime sometimes does prove beneficial, doesn't it?"

"Always willing to give it a shot, you know that, boss."

"Thanks, Christine. Now, go home and enjoy the rest of your evening. Do you want the last piece of pizza?"

She shook her head. "I'll pass on that one. Go for it! I'll see you in the morning."

"I might have a nibble. See you tomorrow."

Sara watched her colleague leave and then munched on the tepid pizza as she mulled over what Christine had come up with. After wiping her hands, she picked up the marker and jotted down on the board as many trades that were likely to have access to different vehicles as she could think of.

Delivery services, garages, the secondhand variety, plus those selling new cars. Although she doubted if the perp would be daft enough to use new cars, she found herself questioning that thought after a while. *What if he's using cars that aren't licenced? With no registered number plate? Could that be the reason why people haven't come forward with a recognised plate number for any of the vehicles?*

She waved the suggestion away. "I'm tired, talking a lot of twaddle and in need of my bed." She entered her office to fetch her jacket and handbag and switched off the light. She passed the whiteboard and reread what she'd just written. She sat at the desk next to the board and tried to add to the list. Then she thumped herself in the head. "Shit! I forgot to check on the woman at the hospital." Picking up the nearby phone, she rang the Accident and Emergency Department. The receptionist took her details and promised that the doctor in charge would get back to her shortly.

In the meantime, she rang Mark to make him aware of the situation and warned him that she wouldn't be home anytime soon.

"You can't stay there all night. You need your rest, love."

"I know. I have an obligation to this woman, she's out there somewhere, who knows what could be happening to her?"

"It's not your responsibility, Sara. Come home. You'll be no good to her if you don't get a decent night's sleep, will you?"

"I know. I'm waiting on the doctor, let me see how that goes. You eat your meal, don't worry about me, I've had pizza. I'm going now, the other phone is ringing. Love you."

"I love you, too."

She ended the call and picked up the phone on the desk. "DI Ramsey."

"Hi, this is Dr Levington. I was asked to ring you."

"Yes, Doctor, thanks for getting back to me. How's the patient?"

"She's unconscious. I've sent her for an MRI scan. I believe she has internal bleeding. Her blood pressure is dropping rapidly; we're keeping her under strict observation right now."

"Thanks. Between you and me, what's your prognosis on this one?"

"I wouldn't normally reveal this. I'm not hopeful. I'm going to stretch my neck out and give her a twenty percent chance of pulling through."

"Shit! Not what I was hoping to hear. Has her next of kin been informed?"

"Of course. Her family are here, waiting for the outcome of the MRI."

"Thank you for informing me. If her condition changes, will you get someone to ring me here ASAP?"

"I will. Goodbye, Inspector."

She replaced the phone and went in search of more coffee. She sat and stared at the whiteboard until Craig and Will entered the incident room half an hour later.

"Anything, guys?"

They both shook their head.

"Nothing much, boss," Craig replied, sounding disheartened.

"Chin up, we're bound to catch a break soon. I've sent the others home. Why don't you guys get off as well?"

"Are you sure?" Will asked.

"Absolutely. Go."

Craig hesitated. "All right if I stay with you, guv?"

She tilted her head. "Any particular reason, Craig?"

"I've got nothing to go home to. I'd be watching dumb TV shows when I could be doing something useful here."

"Go on, then."

"I'm out of here, boss." Will waved and left the room.

"Okay, if you're up for this, then the least I can do is shout you dinner. Name your poison."

Craig shrugged. "Surprise me. Have you eaten?" His nose rose to take in the air. "I smell pizza."

"Nothing wrong with your snout. Yep, Christine and I shared one earlier. Go on, what do you fancy?"

"I don't mind, a pizza will do for me. I can buy my own, you don't have to fork out for it."

"Nonsense, I insist. Place the order, I'll get my card. You haven't got a photographic memory, have you?"

"No. Your card details are safe with me."

Twenty minutes later, Craig was tucking into a pepperoni. Sara swept past his desk and swiped a slice as the aroma was far too tempting not to. She bought them both a coffee, and they discussed the case while he ate.

"Can you think of any other possible businesses which might use different vehicles? I've started the list and was going to ask the team in the morning. Maybe we can get started on the research this evening instead."

He cast his eyes over the list she had created already and then shook his head. "Apart from different types of delivery firms, then no, I can't think of anything useful. Want me to start compiling a list of garages in the area?"

"We'll do it together. Let me ring the desk sergeant, tell him we're likely going to pull an all-nighter."

She rang the front desk.

"Okay, ma'am. If my guys see or hear anything regarding the van, I'll be sure to give you a shout."

"Thanks."

"It's a shame we haven't got the CCTV footage, I could sink my teeth into that." Craig bit into another heavily laden piece of pizza. The cheese slid off the side and onto his desk. "Damn. I'm such a mucky bugger."

Sara sniggered. "You said it. Let me see if I can chase things up on that front." She placed the call, and the man on the other end assured her he'd have the discs for her within the hour.

"That's a bummer," Craig said. "It depends who you get down there. Sometimes they can be a tad stubborn, in my experience."

"Someone needs a clout around the head, that's for sure. At least we'll have something more to keep us occupied." She switched on the TV, realising the news at ten was about to start. After the main news had ended, the local news filled the room, and their case was front and foremost. "Their spin on things always amazes me. Sometimes they work with us—more often than not, they're set against us, though."

"Yeah, that's my take on things, all right. No wonder the police have a bad reputation around here."

"Not good. Let's not dwell on it. At least they've highlighted the abduction and warned the other residents to remain safe and aware at all times. I suppose that saves us trying to get the word out there."

They concentrated their combined efforts and came up with a relatively long list of both used and new car garages within the city limits. Sara pondered whether they should extend the search area but reckoned they could do that later, if they didn't have much success with what they had gathered already.

She breathed out a sigh of relief when the discs were delivered an hour or so later. "You make a start on those, Craig. Let's see if we can crack this overnight."

He chuckled. "No pressure then."

She held her fist up. "We can do this. We're the Superteam, right?"

"If that's what you want to believe, boss, who am I to doubt you?"

"Precisely. More coffee first, though." She bounced out of the chair, feeling more energetic than she should have, given the bloody time, and returned carrying two cups.

"There you go. You're doing well out of me today, I have to say."

He grinned. It was the first time she'd really taken any notice of his handsome features. "Do you have a girlfriend? Gah, tell me to mind my own business if you want to."

"I don't mind, boss. Nah, the last one cheated on me. Said I worked long hours and accused me of ignoring her most of the time."

"I'm sorry. It's tough working the hours we do and having a sustainable relationship. You'll find someone else soon, I'm sure."

"The trick is to stop looking, that's what my mum says."

"I think she's probably right. I had no intention of getting involved again after Philip died." She paused as unexpected tears surfaced. "Anyway, look at me now, planning a second wedding to a totally adorable man."

"You're lucky to have found love a second time. Some of us are still waiting for the hearts and roses the first time."

"Aww...hang in there. What are you, twenty-four, twenty-five?"

"Coming up to twenty-five in a few months. Most of my friends are either married or have a significant other they're living with. Me, I'm in a crummy bachelor pad."

She rubbed the top of his arm. "Don't give up. If my luck can change then there's nothing to say the same thing won't happen to you. Have you tried one of those online dating apps?"

His expression was one of alarm. "Are you kidding me? Don't you think there are enough nutters in the world already? You can't tell me people actually put their real pictures or profiles up on those damn sites."

"I wouldn't know. I suppose you're right. A friend of mine back in Liverpool used a site like that a few years ago, hooked herself a doctor into the bargain after a few months. She's expecting her second child in June. So it can work out for some folks."

"Nope, not for me. I'm not in any rush to settle down. That's what I keep telling myself anyway. Most of the time I believe it."

"Well, any woman will be lucky to have you on her arm. Relax, enjoy yourself and someone will come along soon, I'm sure of it."

"I'm not going to hold my breath. Thanks for your concern, guv. Can we get back to work now? I'm finding the spotlight being on me a little...uncomfortable."

"Sorry. Of course. You should have told me to butt out."

"As if. It's fine, honest."

## 12

*S*ara and Craig worked like trojans until around four. She ordered Craig to go home and not to return at least until one p.m., while she retired to her office and fell asleep at her desk. Carla knocked on the door and woke her from her slumber a few hours later.

"You're kidding me! Please don't tell me you slept here last night?"

Stretching her arms above her head, Sara yawned and confirmed, "Okay, I won't, but I did. I sent Craig home around four."

"Slave driver."

"Don't go flinging that one at me, he volunteered to stay behind and lend me a hand, and you know what? It's surprising how much ground we covered and what results we achieved during the dead of night. Hey, instead of chastising me, a coffee wouldn't go amiss."

Carla peered back over her shoulder into the incident room and tutted. "I'm surprised you slept at all with that amount of caffeine you have pumping around your system."

"Don't judge me." She grinned, stretched the knots out of her spine a second time and jumped out of her chair. She paused to admire the view she found most motivating for a few seconds and then left the office.

The rest of the team were all standing around, enjoying their first vending machine coffee of the day. Even Craig was there.

She wagged her finger in his direction. "How did I know you'd be here early?"

"I suppose I'm easy to read, boss. You're here, so why shouldn't I be?"

"Thanks, Craig."

Carla appeared beside her and deposited a cup in her hand. She sipped at it and then moved towards the whiteboard.

"Listen up gang. Things began to slot into place during the night, at least, we think they have." She pointed out the list she and Craig had pulled together of all the garages in the area selling either new or used cars. "We also made another list of delivery firms in the area. That's all we could think of targeting. If anyone else has a suggestion where the perp could get his hands on different vehicles, we can crack on with making another list today."

"Umm…car or van hire companies perhaps," Will shouted.

Sara pointed a finger in the air. "Plausible. Can you research that for me, Will?"

"Sure. There shouldn't be too many in the area."

"We'll concentrate on Hereford at present. If nothing comes of our research during the day then we'll expand the search area. We're still waiting on Sandra Duck to get back to us, possibly with a name, if she's had the chance to look through Sharon Ryman's case files. But here's the good news. The CCTV Barry ordered last night came into our possession around midnight. Craig and I sifted through the discs, and we believe we found a registration for the van used to abduct Heidi Vickers. We followed that van out of the city, going in the direction of the Rotherwas area."

Carla frowned, and Sara picked her up on it.

"What are you thinking?"

"Doesn't the ex, Tim Davis live in that area?"

Sara nodded, slowly. "You're right. It could be a coincidence, though. So let's not jump to any conclusions just yet. His background checks didn't match anything we've got. I'd rather not get sidetracked at the moment. Let's concentrate on the facts we have to hand for now."

"Okay. I'm going to bear him in mind, though."

Sara relented and jotted down his name and a possible link to the Rotherwas area. "There, it'll be there to remind us, should we draw a blank on this line of enquiry."

"Great." Carla smiled and perched on the desk closest to the whiteboard. "So, did you get the chance to trace the van?"

"We did. It belongs to a Gary Bryson. Carla, you and I will visit the address after we're finished here and once I've filled my veins with caffeine—"

The phone on a nearby desk rang, interrupting her. Carla answered it. Her gaze met Sara's, and she shook her head. Sara crossed the room and craned her neck to listen. She grimaced when Lorraine's dulcet tones filled her ear. Carla handed her the phone.

"Okay, give it to me," Sara said.

"Good morning to you, Inspector. As I was telling your partner, we've got another body."

"Where? I'm hazarding a guess this is Heidi Vickers."

"Your guess is as good as mine at this point with no formal ID present. And you can find us at the lane next to Lossworth Primary School."

"Fuck! It has to be her. She's the headmistress at the school. She was abducted yesterday. Ugh…I'll fill you in when we get there. We're on our way." Sara slammed the phone down, cutting Lorraine off before she had the chance to say anything else. "Right, there's a change of plan. Heidi's body has possibly shown up. I know how upsetting that is for everyone, but I'm asking you all to dig deep and get on with the tasks in hand. Let's do our best to nail this bastard today before he grabs someone else—if there's any other likely candidates on his list, that is."

"Jesus, he's got us running around like crazed animals. What the fuck is his agenda? Why kill a teacher and then the head at the same school?" Carla muttered.

"Let's mull that over on the way. Will and Craig, why don't you take up the reins where Gary Bryson is concerned? Go question him about the vehicle, see if the van is there first... Ugh...you know the drill, you don't need me to tell you how to suck eggs. Christine, will you chase up Sandra Duck for me, around tennish? That should give her enough time to get something organised by then."

"Will do, boss."

"The rest of you keep on with the background checks, and Barry, you can make a list of the car and van hire outlets in the area while we're gone."

"I'm on it, guv."

"Come on, Carla, sup up and we'll get going."

*L*orraine was standing next to her vehicle. The pathway had been cordoned off, and there was a small cluster of nosey onlookers at either end.

"Jesus, what is wrong with people?" Sara snarled as she and Carla approached the pathologist.

Lorraine shrugged. "Ah, morbid fascination. It makes the world go round, don't you know?"

"I thought that was money," Sara replied, confused.

"You've got your perception and I've got mine."

"Whatever. Let's see her."

"My guys have just finished erecting the marquee, we should be good to go."

"Carla, you stay here and start shifting these people back. Unless there's a witness amongst them, they have no right to be here."

"I'll ask the pertinent question and move their arses if they don't provide an adequate response." She marched away, resembling an artillery soldier on a mission.

"How come you think you know the victim?" Lorraine asked.

They walked the few feet to the tent after Sara had slipped on her protective clothing and shoes. They entered, and Sara stared down at the victim.

"That's her. We got a call from a witness to say Heidi, the head-mistress at the primary school, and victim one's boss, had been abducted and that another woman had done her best to try to intervene and got mown down by the van in the process."

"Shit! Is she all right?"

"Nope, she's in hospital. Damn, I was supposed to check on her this morning. I've been at work all night, concerned for Heidi's safety. I needn't have bloody bothered. Any idea of time of death?"

"Hard to tell. Possibly between eight and ten last night."

"And she was dumped here then?"

"Maybe. Heck, I don't know, the dampness to her hair tells me she was more than likely killed in the same manner as the other two vics, except not as harshly as vic two."

"Back up, you think she was drowned, just not electrocuted then, right?"

"Yep, that sums it up and what I said."

"We'll agree to differ on that one. I might not have heard you correctly."

"Intriguing turn of events nevertheless. Are you any further forward with the investigation?"

"We're getting there. This one has stretched us to our limits every day. The perp is cagey and aware of how to make life awkward for us, that's my prediction anyway."

"Sounds like it. Three victims in less than a week, that's—"

"Don't say it, serial killer territory. I'm aware of that and the urgency behind getting the shit off the streets, but if the clues aren't there, well, you know as well as I do, our hands are tied securely until we catch a break."

"I wasn't having a pop at you, only stating the obvious. You look done in."

"I'm knackered but I'll plod on. I have a deep-rooted sensation that our paths are going to cross soon enough."

"I hope you're right. What else do you need to know?"

"You tell me, you're the bloody expert... Sorry to snap. What about if there was any possible DNA left on the body?"

"No. Maybe that's why he drowns them, although he then has to move them to dump them, so ignore that suggestion. What we do have is possible contusions that occurred post mortem."

Lorraine crouched, and Sara joined her. She pointed out several patches at the front and back of the victim's head and neck.

"Ouch, pretty brutal, hateful even."

"Yep, it's as though he was punishing her for dying on him, as though he wasn't ready to let her go quite yet."

"Sadistic shit. He intended to torture her longer, is that what you're saying?"

"Conceivably. Purely speculation for now."

"What if he was angry at her dying? What if all he wanted to do was to scare her, and the other vics, come to that?"

"It's a possibility. Who knows, except the killer, of course, what ran through his mind after he'd abducted the women? One thing is for sure, his hatred for either the woman or the situation of her dying, reared its ugly head when he carried out the kicking."

Sara cringed and shuddered. "Kicking? Fuck, I never even thought of that."

"Anyway, let's get the scene processed. I wanted you here first thing. Once we're done, I'm going to get her shifted ASAP. I hate the thought of the little ones knowing, let alone seeing, a dead body out here."

"The dead body of their own headmistress to boot," Sara added sullenly. "I suppose my next job should be to inform the husband. I'm not looking forward to that, he's a bloody solicitor."

"There are days when I don't envy you in the slightest."

"Thanks. Send the PM report through when you can."

"You've got it."

Sara left the tent and walked back to join Carla who was resting against the car. Sara stripped off her protective suit, flung it in the boot and then jumped in. "Dare I ask how you got on?"

"Appallingly, if you must know. Not a single hint of anyone seeing anything. They're all here for a good gawp, sick shits!"

"Human nature at its finest."

"Was the vic killed the same way?"

"As in drowned, yes. There's also a lot of bruising around her face and neck. Lorraine is proposing the killer attacked her after she'd died on him. Possibly kicked the shit out of her."

"That's bloody bizarre. Any hint as to why?"

"We bounced a few ideas around. Because she probably died on him earlier than he was anticipating. Maybe he wanted to punish her further and attacked her just for the sake of it. Something we need to ask him, if and when we catch him."

"We'll catch him all right. It's only a matter of time before he slips up and we nab him, isn't it?"

"I'd like to think so. Do me a favour, look up Taylor, Johnson and Metcalfe for me. See if Karl Vickers is at work today. It'll be quicker to do that than trawl out to his house in the back of beyond, only to find he's not there. I'll head in that direction."

Carla made the call and gave Sara the thumbs-up. They pulled into the solicitor's car park around ten minutes later. Sara inhaled and exhaled a few times, preparing herself for what lay ahead of her, and then left the vehicle with Carla not far behind her.

The receptionist was a man in his early thirties. He smiled and asked, "Hi, can I help you?"

Sara and Carla produced their IDs, and Sara asked, "We'd like a chat with Mr Vickers, if he's free?"

"He's with a client at present." He glanced up at the clock on the wall and then at his computer screen. "He shouldn't be too long now. Why don't you take a seat? Can I get you a drink while you wait?"

"No, we're fine. Thanks."

They sat in the comfy orange chairs bathed in the morning sun. A few minutes later, Karl Vickers emerged from one of the offices and accompanied an elderly woman, dressed in a smart tartan suit to the front door. He shook her hand and bid her farewell, and all the while his gaze was locked on Sara's.

"Hello there. Have you found her?"

Sara swallowed down the bile burning her throat. "Maybe we should talk in your office, sir."

His hopeful expression gave way to a stormy one, and he gestured for them to join him in his office. The three of them stepped inside and took a seat each.

"It's not good news, is it? Is she in hospital? Don't tell me it's worse than that, please?"

"I'm sorry, Mr Vickers. This morning, Heidi's body was found close to the school."

He covered his eyes with one hand and said over and over, "Oh my God, oh my God. This can't be true. Not Heidi."

Sara and Carla glanced at each other, each of them misty-eyed.

Sara then huffed out a breath. "I'm sorry. It's not the outcome we were hoping for. We did our best."

His hand dropped, and he glared at her. "If you'd done your best, my wife would still be alive, Inspector, wouldn't she?"

"My team and I have worked through the night. We didn't have any clues to go on. I'm sorry, please be assured that—"

"Assured? How can I be assured about anything you're likely to tell me? I've heard enough. I think you'd better leave now. You failed me. More importantly, you failed Heidi by not finding her before this madman killed her. I'm presuming *he* did kill her? She didn't drop down dead with a heart attack, did she?"

"No, sir. I mean, yes, she was murdered. You have our condolences and my personal assurance that I won't rest—"

"Until the culprit is found, right? Did you give the same spiel to the other victims' families?"

"I understand you lashing out at me like this…I can't apologise enough for letting you down. Letting Heidi down. I will bring this person to justice. On that, you have my word."

"Get out. And don't come back until you have this person in custody, you hear me?" he shouted and pointed at the door.

Sara and Carla didn't hang around. They left the building as if there were hot coals under their feet.

"That was bloody harsh," Carla announced as they walked towards the car.

"He had a right to be angry. We let him down."

"Even so. You and Craig worked all night long. He wasn't prepared to listen, though."

"Would you, if you were in his shoes? Leave it, Carla. Let's not dwell on it." She drove on autopilot back to the station, reliving the horrible event that had just taken place. She understood that victims' spouses had a right to vent their anger, but she and her team had been working non-stop on trying to find the killer on this one. They were just as exasperated as the family members were, if not more, in fact.

However, once they were back at the station their spirits were lifted by the news Christine had for them all.

"Sandra Duck has finally given us a name, boss. A Jason Campbell."

"Tell me you have more than that."

"I do. I'm in the process of piecing it all together now."

Just then, Craig and Will entered the incident room. Sara spun on her heel and eyed them expectantly.

Craig cleared his throat and said, "Gary Bryson exchanged the van about a month ago. The documentation hasn't been updated with Swansea yet."

"Bugger. Do we know where he exchanged the van?"

"Yep, it was at a garage on our list, boss." Craig beamed, probably sensing, as Sara did, that the net was closing in, finally.

Sara held up a finger and faced Christine again. "You were saying? Tell me you have an address for him."

"I have a former address for him, if that will help, boss. Nothing on the system for a recent address, though. And yes, he's a car salesman who owns his own business out near Rotherwas."

Sara punched the air with both hands. "Yes, yes, yes. Okay, let's calm down and try and connect all the dots before we get too carried away. Did Sandra say anything else, Christine?"

"She went through the whole sorry story. His former girlfriend kicked him out of his home two years ago. They have a five-year-old son. He's been fighting constantly to be a part of his life ever since. The former girlfriend has done everything she can to prevent that from happening."

"Shit! So he's taking the law into his own hands. Killing off those who have prevented him from having any contact with his son. It all makes sense. It's extreme, but putting yourself in his shoes, if he's crying out to be part of his son's life and those in authority are doing their utmost to stop that, how would you feel? Where's the girlfriend now?"

"Apparently, she's running a pub in Bristol, well, that's the last Sandra heard."

"How long has she been there? It doesn't matter, get the name of the pub, see if she's still in residence there."

"She's been there for around ten months."

Sara scratched her face. "It doesn't make sense. Surely the son wouldn't have attended the school in Hereford if he lived in Bristol, would he?"

Christine shrugged. "I wouldn't have thought so."

Carla tutted. "Something has tipped him over the edge. Maybe he's killing off everyone who has let him down in the *past*, not the present."

"Okay. That makes sense. Let's get digging, see if anything is showing up through the family court system to give us a clue."

"Sorry, Craig, Will, I need you to go to his place of work. We'll put him under surveillance for now, especially as we have no known address for him."

The two detectives raced out of the incident room as fast as Sara's heart was pumping blood through her veins. She raised the fingers of her right hand and nibbled on her nails, one by one.

Carla nudged her, drawing Sara's gaze away from the whiteboard. "Hey, what's going on?"

"We're so close now. I'm worried in case we screw things up."

"There's no chance of that happening, not with you in charge."

"Ha, I wish I shared your confidence."

"Boss." Christine waved to get her attention.

Sara shot across the room to stand beside her. "What is it?"

Christine held the phone out to her, her finger poised ready to connect Sara with a mystery person she presumed was on the other end of the line. "Who is it?"

"Wayne Loddon. He runs the pub in Bristol." Her mouth twisted. "I think you need to speak with him. Er…he's what I would call seething."

"Why?"

"Because I dared to mention Jenna Wallace's name, Campbell's ex."

"Thanks for the warning. Here goes." Sara cleared her throat and nodded at Christine to connect them. "Mr Loddon?"

"That's right. Hey, I don't appreciate someone from the cop shop ringing me up asking impertinent questions and then bloody leaving me on hold."

"I apologise. No harm meant. My colleague had trouble tracking me down. Are you free for a quick chat?"

"It depends. How quick? I have the draymen due any moment now, and there's only me to take care of the deliveries. Make that there's only me here to see to everything now that bitch has taken off."

"I gather you're talking about Jenna Wallace?"

"That's right. Drug-taking bloody whore."

*Nice way to speak about your former partner.*

"Perhaps you can tell me about your relationship, Mr Loddon?"

"It's Wayne. Where do I begin?"

"I find at the beginning always works best."

"Yeah, right. Like I said, I ain't got long, and it's quite a lengthy story, so I'd prefer it if you didn't interrupt."

"I can't guarantee that. Let's see how things progress first, shall we?"

Sara perched on the desk behind her and put the phone on speaker for the others to hear. She listened to him take a swig of his drink, let out a small belch and then begin. She rolled her eyes at Christine and mouthed 'Pig'.

"So, well, it all began when she was seeing this other fella. Actually, she was living with him at the time. We thought we'd meet up for a bit of a giggle behind the bloke's back."

"This fella would be Jason Campbell, I take it?"

"That's right… As I was saying, well, things got serious, and well, we fell in love. At least I thought it was love at the time. She told me he beat her up and she was petrified of him. I fell for her story, you know, hook, line and stinker. Yeah, I know I've said that wrong, you'll see why I said *stinker* as the story unfolds."

"You started seeing each other, and what next?"

"I helped her clear the house of all her possessions. She told me she'd paid for everything. I learned later that this Jason was up to his neck in debt because of this bitch. Everything that fell out of her mouth was a frigging lie, even down to her telling me she loved me. Anyway, we moved all her stuff into my gaff and then we searched around for this place; she told me she fancied running a pub. I agreed, and the rest is history."

"And the son? What happened to him?"

"He got dragged along for the ride."

"Did you care for him?"

"Yeah, like he was my own. Well, she didn't have a clue what to do with him. It later transpired that she preferred to do as little as possible during the day. That included seeing to her son's needs. She told me a few times to put Kenzie in the dog's cage. That's what she used to do when she was with Jason, so it turns out."

"Really? Did you ever witness her abusing the boy?"

"Verbally, now and then. When the pub was busy, she would lock him in his bedroom at night. I told her it was wrong to do that. Pointed out that he could get trapped if there's a bloody fire. She waved my concerns away. Anyway, the customers got to hear about it because she has a big mouth and seemed proud of the way she was treating her son. That's when the trouble began really. Your lot showed up, tore us off a strip. It didn't stop her, though. You know what she feeds that kid of hers?"

"No, we don't really know much about either her or her son, so we're relying on you to tell us. Go on."

"She opens a can of either beans or spaghetti hoops and gives him a fork. In the dead of winter, too. Poor kid. I tried giving him healthy meals, but she had a right go at me for feeding him properly."

"Did she say why?"

"She knew best how to treat her son, apparently."

"And what about the father? What can you tell me about him?"

"Poor guy. She screwed him over big time. Worse still, she lied over and over about him to the authorities. I met him the once, when we cleared the house out; he showed up and kicked up a fuss. The cops told him to get out of there or he would have been arrested. The thing is, everyone comes down on the mother's side, even when they're a piece of trash like her. She's carrying my kid now."

"I see. I take it you're now separated, is that correct?"

"Yep. She stole money from the pub, wages meant for the staff. Then we fell out, and she blackmailed me. Dragged the nipper out of his bed at four o'clock in the morning, stole my car with the spare set of keys and blackmailed me for ten grand in exchange for the car. Sick, she is. That Jason is well shot of her, except he isn't. He took her to court for access to his son. He got it, too, but he had to go through a number of supervised visits before the court allowed him proper access. Then they said he could have one weekend in three with the little man. He was thrilled, over the moon to have contact with Kenzie again, but her cunning mind went to work. She told him she wanted funds out of the house she left him with. The poor chap had to come up with twenty grand to pay her off. He remortgaged the house just to get shot of her. The weekend visits went according to plan for months until Jason paid her that damn money."

"And what happened then?"

"She took off. Left me, took the kid and ran."

"Has Jason tried to contact you?"

"Yeah, we had a chat. I apologised for playing a part in breaking them up. He said he didn't care about that, all he wanted now was to get his son back. The bloke is going out of his mind. He's supposed to have two FaceTime chats with his son every week; he's had nothing for months now. I told him I would do all I could to help him, but she's a devious cu...umm, devious scumbag, who likes nothing better than to have a hold over a man. I told him she's pregnant again. I'm taking her through the courts as soon as that kid makes an appearance in this world. There's no way she's going to be in charge of that kid's welfare. Jason has taken her back to court in the last few months for breaking the court order. She hasn't showed up at court. The magistrates are the bloody pits. Again, they're siding with this evil, conniving bitch. I wish I could do more to help him, but well…at the end of the day, she manipulates people's way of thinking, especially those in authority. That boy deserves to be with his father, who loves and cares for him. He was the significant parental caregiver when they were together, not her. The system is so fucking screwed up, though."

"That's unfortunate. Do you know where Jenna is now?"

"No. Like I said, as soon as that twenty grand hit her bank account, she took off. My bet is that she's started up at a new pub somewhere. I've got my ear to the ground, and the minute I find out where she is, I'm going to make some waves with the brewery. I dread to think who is looking after that poor kid now that I'm not around. She couldn't give a damn about him, that much is evident. Kenzie is just a chess piece in one of her games. Uh-oh, there's the draymen pulling into the yard now. Sorry, I can't help you any more. If you catch up with her, tell her she deserves all that's coming to her."

"Excuse me? Hello, Wayne? Are you still there?" He was gone. "Shit, if I didn't know any better, I'd say he was privy to what was going on, possibly willing Jason on," Sara noted.

"Let's bring him in then," Carla suggested.

"Hold fire on that thought. What if he can lead us to Jason?" Placing her fingertips on each side of her temple, Sara massaged the area in circles. "Bloody hell. That poor man."

"What? Are you crazy?" Carla shouted. "You can't take the law into your own hands like that."

"I know. I didn't mean that he was within his rights to exact revenge on those who had failed him, but, bloody hell, his whole life as he knew it, has been ripped apart by people in authority letting him and, more importantly, his little lad down. All I'm saying is that, well, sometimes the law is an ass. Why couldn't the judges, Social Services and the school see that all he was trying to do was to get his lawful visiting rights with his son? That kiddie must be so confused. To have a loving father like that torn from his life and to be living with a mother, who obviously couldn't give a damn shit about him."

Carla shook her head and looked annoyed. "It still doesn't make what he's done right."

"Believe me, I know that. I can sympathise with him, that's all I'm saying. Shit, there are fathers out there who walk away from all responsibility. Surely he's doing his best to try to remain in contact with his son, and yet she's doing everything possible to ensure they stay separated. What's right about that?"

"But murder?"

Sara held up her hands. "Three murders, I'm aware of all of them."

"And yet, here you are, apparently standing in his corner?"

"I was doing nothing of the sort. All I was trying to do was approach things objectively."

"I'm sorry, but we'll have to agree to differ on this one." Carla marched back to her desk, threw herself in her chair and folded her arms, her expression one of sheer anger.

Sara knew she hadn't conveyed her views very well. She was exhausted, and that had played a part in her getting the wrong words out. She walked over to Carla and lowered her voice so the others couldn't hear. "Don't think badly of me, partner. It came out all wrong. Lack of sleep can do that to a person."

"You can make all the excuses under the sun, Sara. The fact that you virtually gave Jason Campbell the green light to become a serial killer is, well, sickening."

Sara sighed, and her cheeks puffed out. "Well, if you put it like that, then yes, you're right. I know what I meant, and it wasn't that. I was just trying to put the point across that when the system fails someone and destroys their lives, where is that someone supposed to turn, when, with the best will in the world, all that person is trying to do is protect the one person they love most in this life?"

"There you go again, defending his motives."

Sara growled. "I'm not, I swear I'm not. God, have some compassion for the poor man, Carla. I hope you never find yourself in such a cruel situation…"

Carla just stared at her open-mouthed for what seemed like eons. In the end, Sara shrugged and turned to concentrate on the whiteboard once more. She'd never fallen out with her partner; had she done that this time? All they had were opposing views on a suspect who happened to be quite important.

Her head pounded the more she tried to figure things out. She retired to her office and closed the door behind her. Without realising what she was doing, she picked up her mobile and rang Mark's number.

"Hello, stranger. How's it going down there?"

"Hi, I needed to hear a friendly voice."

"Sounds ominous. Is everything all right?"

"Yeah, it's fine. Just a misunderstanding between the troops, nothing that we won't be able to put right in a few hours. I missed you last night."

"Hey, you're not the only one. The bed felt empty. The whole house did, in fact, without you being there."

"Did Misty miss me?"

"I believe she did. She sat by the front door all evening. I took her up to bed with me, and she seemed to settle down then."

Her heart tugged. "It's nice to be appreciated. I'm sorry I didn't make it back home. I think we're in for a hectic day."

"How so?"

"We think we know who the killer is, we've just got to track the bastard down now."

"That's great news. I have every faith in you and the team."

"I wish I had half as much. I'll see you later. Shall we get a take-away tonight?"

"No, I should finish early. Damn, there goes my surprise. I'll cook us a nice meal. Did you even eat last night?"

"Yeah, greasy pizza that repeated on me all night long. I'll see you later, love you."

"Right backatcha, beautiful."

She hung up, a broad smile stretching her lips apart. Sara then got down to tackling the morning post. She'd rather be holed up in her office than be in a frosty atmosphere in the incident room. She resurfaced at around twelve, her tummy rumbling, complaining that it had been hours since it had been treated to any form of nourishment.

The team were hard at it, as usual. Carla intentionally kept her head down, even though Sara knew she'd seen her come out of the office.

"Okay, who fancies some lunch? I'm buying."

Four hands shot up, but Carla ignored the question.

"Carla?"

"No, thanks. Not hungry."

"Suit yourself. Anyone fancy a trip to the baker's?"

"I'll go," Marissa shot out of her chair.

"Here's twenty. I fancy a brown chicken roll if they have one."

Marissa took the orders and left the room. The atmosphere chilled Sara to the bone. She shrugged and went back to her office. She contacted Craig and Will to see how things stood on the stakeout.

"Hi, boss. Nothing, absolutely zilch happening here," Craig replied, sounding downbeat.

"As in, there are no customers?"

"As in, the place is bloody closed. The gates are locked. We've managed to spot some of the vehicles he's used in the crimes, though, so that's an added bonus. What do you want us to do?"

"Can you find a way in? He could be hiding out inside. We need to be sure he isn't doing that."

"I could climb the fence. Will the force cover the cost of me ripping my trousers in the process?"

She chuckled. "Yep, go on. Let me know how you get on. We can't find a known address for him. I'm thinking he might be living on site. Be careful, Craig."

"I will. Get back to you soon."

Carla suddenly burst into her office without knocking.

Startled, Sara stared at her and hung up. "What's going on?"

"We need to go. He's abducted someone else."

"Shit!" She scrambled out of her chair and yanked her jacket off the back. "Do we know who?"

"You'll find out when we get there."

"Fuck, Carla, don't play games with me."

"His solicitor."

"Jesus Christ."

## 13

Karl Vickers had blood trickling down his head from a wound.

"Karl, what's going on?" Sara asked, tearing out of the car with Carla in hot pursuit behind her.

"He was here. He's taken her. I tried to stop him. He beat me over the head with a bar. I couldn't help her. I desperately wanted to…but I couldn't stop him from taking her."

"Sorry, who has he taken?"

"Nikki Murphy. She's his solicitor. He was here shouting the odds not long before that. Shariff and I tried to placate him, but he wasn't having any of it. He left. It was clear he was still angry. Nikki had nipped out to the shops in her lunch hour, and when she came back, he jumped her. I happened to be looking out of the window. I shot out of the office to confront him; Shariff tried to help as well. He attacked us with a bar. Nikki was out cold. I don't know what he did to her, but she was out cold in the back of his ruddy car."

"His car? Did you get the reg?" Carla asked.

"Shariff did. He's inside, he's beside himself. Nikki is his ex-wife."

"Bugger. Okay, here, let me help you stand up. We need to get you to the hospital."

"No, I need to stay here. I have appointments."

"I can't allow you to do that, Karl, not with a head injury."

"I must, and you shouldn't be here. You have to go after him. Don't let him…kill her, like he did Heidi."

"We're going to do our best. I'm going to ring for an ambulance."

"Don't! I wouldn't want to waste their time. Shariff will take me to the hospital, he's injured as well."

"Good. I need to speak with him. Where is he?" She helped Karl through the main entrance, and they found another suited man with sun-kissed skin inside.

"Mate. This is Inspector Ramsey, she's dealing with Heidi's case. Tell her what you know."

The man nodded. "Shariff Dunmore. He shoved Nikki in the back of a dark-blue Alfa Romeo, HY 89 DOR. We tried to save her, honest we did. He beat us back." Shariff held his hand against the side of his head, and when he took it away, it was covered in blood.

"Carla, get Mr Dunmore to a seat, quickly."

Carla helped him over to one of the orange chairs in reception, and Sara assisted Karl to the same area. Both men stared at each other and shook their injured heads.

"Why? Why is he doing this?" Karl asked.

"We believe it's a custody battle gone wrong. You say that Nikki is his solicitor?"

"That's right, for the past two years. I've worked with her on the case. Never expected it to blow up in our faces like this."

"Has Jason Campbell ever shown any signs of aggression towards either of you before?" Sara asked.

"No, not at all. Well, maybe the conversations have become heated once his frustration has shown; we accept that most of the time. His face, he seemed deranged. All I could think of was that he'd killed Heidi and the red mist descended. I did my best to try and keep Nikki safe, but it was like he had superhuman strength. Please, you have to get out there and find him."

"We're doing our best. We're struggling to find a known address for him. Perhaps you can tell us if you have one on file?"

"Paul, get me the Campbell file out of Nikki's office, will you?" Karl instructed the guy on reception.

He shot out of his chair and reappeared a few seconds later carrying a thick file. He handed it to Karl and backed up. Karl flicked open the front cover and tapped his finger. He read out an address which Carla jotted down in her notebook.

"Thanks, do we know if anyone else lives there? Could it be his parents' address perhaps?"

"I can't tell you that."

"Come on, gents. We need to get you to hospital," Sara pleaded.

"No. What you need to do is stop worrying about us and get out there and find him. One of our colleagues will pop next door to the doctor's surgery, see if they can assist us. Please, just go."

"If you're sure? Okay, I'll give you a ring later, as soon as we locate him."

Sara and Carla raced out to the car.

"Don't say it," she warned Carla. She could tell by the look she was giving her that an 'I told you so' was on the cards.

"I'll keep my mouth shut because—"

Sara's raised hand stopped her from saying anything else. "Get Craig or Will on the phone while I drive."

They jumped in the car, and Sara sped out of the car park.

Craig answered the phone, "Yes, boss. I climbed the fence but couldn't see anything."

"Never mind. He's kidnapped someone else. I need you to be aware of that, he might come back there. He's driving a dark-blue Alfa Romeo, HY 89 DOR."

"Damn. Sorry to hear that. Right, we'll keep a lookout for it and get back to you."

"Good. Stay safe. Ring me ASAP." She nodded for Carla to end the call. "We need to get back to base, see if we can trace the car on the ANPR system. God, I feel so bloody useless. We have to find him before he kills her."

"Want to hear how I would proceed?"

Sara glanced her way, frowning. "Go on."

"I'd remain on the streets. Get the team on the ANPRs, that way, we can arrive at a location promptly. Time is going to be a considerable factor here, after all."

"Okay, do it. Ring the station, get the ball rolling. I'm going to head towards the Rotherwas area, that seems to be a key place for him."

Carla rang the station to action the plan and hung up. "I'm sorry for falling out with you earlier."

"There's no need for you to apologise. Please bear in mind that in no way was I sticking up for Campbell. My intention was to play devil's advocate, that's all. There's no way I would condone him going on a damn killing spree."

"Okay. Friends again." Carla offered up her pinky finger.

Sara linked it with hers and laughed. "You're nuts. Let's hope we find him soon, eh?"

"Yeah, judging by what has gone on in the past, it doesn't bode well."

Sara turned the car around and drove through town, round the Asda roundabout and then took a left, signposted Rotherwas not long after. "Where could he take her? The place must have some form of water source."

"I don't know. There are a few rivers down this way. It flooded back in February."

"But then so did most of Hereford. Isn't Rotherwas known for being a trading estate?"

"That's right. There aren't many residential homes in that area. Here maybe, but not once you get farther into the district. What are you thinking?"

"I don't know. A disused factory, warehouse even? Something along those lines."

"Okay, let me bring up Google Maps, see what I can find. They're regenerating the area, pulling down all the old buildings and erecting new energy-efficient ones."

"Sounds promising, go with that. It's not far now, is it?"

"Two minutes up the road before the actual trading estate starts.

This end is where I think we should be concentrating our efforts on."

The trading estate came into view up ahead. Sara, under Carla's and Google Maps' guidance, took the first road on the right. Several other roads soon branched off.

"Jesus, I've come past here a few times, you know, to go to the tip. Never realised there was so much here. It's mind-blowing."

"It's also a good place to hide out, right?"

Sara nodded and took a right turn. This led up to the back of the estate. Some of the buildings seemed to be past their usefulness. She continued down the road. The farther they travelled, the worse the buildings' state of repair got. The final building loomed. She pulled up outside and craned her neck.

"What's that?" She pressed back against the seat and pointed to the area near the rear of the building.

"What?" Carla leaned forward.

"I'm going to take a look. There's something back there."

"Wait. Let me call for backup. Craig and Will are just up the road."

"You do that. I'm going in there."

Carla grasped her arm. "Be careful."

Sara winked at her. "Careful is my middle name, hon." She exited the vehicle and quietly closed the door so as not to alert anyone of her arrival. She snuck around the side of the building, avoiding the shards of metal sticking out from its dilapidated exterior and the rubble blocking the pathway that lead to the rear. *Shit! I was right, there's a frigging car here.* The closer she got, the more she was drawn to the dark vehicle. It dawned on her that it was the car they were after.

Turning, she waved emphatically at Carla and gave her the thumbs-up. Then she continued on her journey. She extracted her pepper spray and tucked it up the sleeve of her jacket. Voices emanated from inside. Someone was speaking—no, shouting. A male voice. A female's whimpering, almost sobbing voice filtered through the hole in the façade that used to house a window at one time.

Sara's heartbeat thundered in her ears. She had to get in there and quickly, but how? What if presenting herself forced him to kill the woman?

The decision was taken away from her when the male popped his head through a window casing not two feet ahead of her. "I know you're out there. Come in, join us. The more the merrier."

"Jason, let's talk about this."

"Get in here *now*. Or I'll slice her to pieces."

"I'm coming. Don't do anything you're likely to regret."

He laughed at that. "I'd say it was too late for that."

Sara entered the rear of the property to find who she presumed was Nikki Murphy tied to a plank of wood, her legs dangling into an old oil drum. "Are you okay, Nikki?"

"Yes, please, help me," the solicitor sobbed.

"Please help me," Jason mimicked cruelly. "And where the fuck were you when *I* needed help?" He spun to face Sara and pointed at Nikki. "She's a thieving cow. Do you know how much this fucking bitch has cost me for her incompetent advice over the past two years?"

"I charged you the going rate. I didn't pocket the money, if that's what you're thinking."

"The going rate, that's a frigging laugh, and where has it got me? Eh? Twenty-eight grand poorer, and still that treacherous whore has my son."

*Ouch! Twenty-eight grand! No wonder he's livid, bitter at the way people have let him down.*

"All right, Jason, look, now that I'm aware of your case, let me see what I can do to help you. Give me the chance to put some things right."

"It's too late for that. She's the last one. Then I'm going after that slag. I'll kill both of them if I have to."

"Both of them? Nikki and Jenna, is that who you mean?"

"Yes, then I'll take my son and leave the country. All I ever wanted was to protect and love that boy. And all she's ever done is stand in the way." He prodded Nikki in the arm.

"I didn't. My hands were tied. The court system favours the mothers in cases such as this."

"Ha! Even though the authorities have proof that she isn't a fit mother, she still has sole custody of my child. I have no rights. My name is on his birth certificate, but it means fuck all. Do you know how much I frigging pay that slapper a month in maintenance?"

Sara shook her head at the same time Nikki dipped hers.

"You know, go on, tell her." Jason jabbed Nikki in the stomach, winding her for a moment.

"Nearly five hundred pounds," Nikki choked out the words.

"Can you believe *that*? I know it's supposed to be for my son, but fucking hell, when you see the type of meals she gives him, you can't help but wonder where that money is going, because she ain't spending it on my child, for fuck's sake. Is it any wonder I'm losing my mind and have been driven to doing all this?"

"I can't apologise enough for the system lacking and failing you the way it has, please, won't you allow me to help you?"

He glared at Sara and moved closer to Nikki. "I'm warning you, don't effing treat me like a bloody idiot."

Sara raised her hands. The can slid up her arm, and she lowered them again. The can slipped back into her palm but remained covered by her sleeve. "No tricks. I promise. Let Nikki go. I'm more valuable than her. Take me as your hostage and set her free."

"Why? She deserves to be punished, you don't, not yet."

"Come on. That's it, keep talking to me. Let's try and work together, Jason. I have influences I can lean on to make things better for you."

His eyes narrowed. "Don't mess with me and don't talk bullshit. You think she hasn't got influences?"

"Nikki's hands were tied with the courts, mine won't be. Won't you give me a chance to make amends for their mistakes?"

"The only thing that will put things right is if I see my son again. You know she's moved, don't you? Up sticks. I haven't been told where she is. I was due to have Kenzie for half-term. She didn't show up at the allotted drop-off point. Two court cases later, where she was a no-show and I'm no further forward, and you know what this one said?" He jabbed his fingers in Nikki's stomach a second time. "She more or less shrugged as though me having contact with my son didn't frigging matter. Well, I'll show her how much it matters." With one eye on Sara, he yanked on the chain, and Nikki was lowered slowly into the water.

"Do something. Help me! Don't let him kill me like the others. Please, stop…" Nikki's voice was cut off as her head sank beneath the surface.

"Jason, listen to me. Don't do this. She's not worth it. No one is worth it. I can help you if you'll give me the chance. Tell me what to do," Sara pleaded.

He paused for a moment and then winched Nikki back out of the water. She coughed, her lungs obviously filled with water.

"Help me!" she spluttered, her dripping wet hair plastered to her face.

"Get Kenzie here," Jason said.

"What? Do you know where he is?"

"No. That's the trouble. No one knows where he is."

Sara raked a hand through her hair. "Damn. All I can do is try and find him, but that's going to take time."

A demonic grin appeared, and his gaze flicked between Nikki and Sara. "How long do you think she's gonna stand being dunked in freezing cold water?"

"I can't stand it, not again, please do something," Nikki implored, staring at Sara.

"Give me something to work with, Nikki. Where is she?" Sara asked.

"I don't know. How should I know? All I have is an email address for her and a phone number. They're back at the office."

Sara raised a finger at Jason. "Give me half an hour. Promise me you won't hurt her."

He nodded. "No tricks," he warned.

"You have my word. I'm going to the car now, I'll be back, soon."

"Thirty minutes, not a minute longer."

Sara set the timer on her watch and ran back to the car. Breathlessly, she dived into the driver's seat just as Craig and Will pulled up. She motioned for them to join her, and while she rang Nikki's workplace, she hurriedly explained the situation to her three colleagues.

"You can't bring the child here," Carla objected.

"I'm hoping it won't come to that. The poor bloke only wants to speak to him."

"You just told us he wants him here. Don't mess with him, Sara," Carla said.

"You're right. I should do as he says and put the child in jeopardy."

Carla's chest puffed out. "There's no need for you to be sarcastic."

"Then stop bloody pulling against me. If you haven't got anything productive or useful to say, shut up."

Carla folded her arms and stared out of the side window. Sara spoke to Karl Vickers, apprised him of the situation and requested the information she was after from Jason's file. He came back on the line not long after with the details which Sara noted down in her notebook.

"Please, don't let him hurt Nikki," Karl urged.

"I'm doing all I can. I have to go. Keep us all in your thoughts."

Sara ended the call and swivelled in her seat to face Craig and Will. "Any suggestions?"

"Well, there are four of us and one of him," Craig pointed out.

"There is that. He doesn't know you two are here, or Carla for that matter."

Her partner faced her. "Count me out. I ain't going anywhere near that madman."

Sara raised an eyebrow. "If I give the order, you'll jump to it, you hear me? Cut the attitude, matey."

"I have an injured partner who I'm caring for at home. I can't afford to get involved in shit like this."

"Fair enough. I'll let you off this time. Craig, are you up for tackling him?"

"I'll give it a go, boss. Did you get a good look at the inside? Did you spot any other way to get in there?"

"I'm sure there was a doorway off to the right at the back. It would be a risk."

"One I'm willing to take. What about you, Will?"

The older man shrugged. "I'm game. I can sit on him once Craig's made his move."

The others chuckled at the image his remark conjured up.

"Glad to know you'll be of use somewhere along the line, Will. Right, I have the information I need. I'm going back in there. I'll leave you guys to sort things out here. Don't be too far behind me. If I manage to contact his son, it could be the distraction we need to jump him. Okay?"

She left the car and made her way back inside. Jason was in Nikki's face, still venting his anger on her.

"I'm here. I've got the details. Let's see if we can make contact with Jenna, right, Jason?"

"Go on then. You can try. I'll stay here and get ready to dunk dear Nikki if you fail."

"No, please," Nikki whined, her teeth chattering now from the cold.

"Ha, hypothermia will be setting in soon, you'd better hurry up. The others never got the chance to get cold."

"I'm doing my best. I'm dialling the number now."

"Hello, who's that?" a young boy answered the phone.

"Hello, is that Kenzie?" Sara asked, her gaze fixed on Jason, his eyes expanding at the mention of his son's name.

"Is it him?" Jason whispered.

Sara nodded. "Kenzie, I have someone who wants to speak to you. Hold on." She stepped forward, encouraging Jason to take the phone.

Beyond him, she spotted Craig appearing in the doorway on the other side. Nikki gasped. Sara closed the gap between herself and Nikki and laid a hand on her shoulder.

"It's okay, stay calm, we'll get you free soon," she whispered in Nikki's ear.

"Son, son, is that you?"

"Daddy, is that my daddy?"

Sara's vision misted over. Kenzie sounded so thrilled to hear his daddy's voice. Her heart went out to both of them.

"I love you, Kenzie. How have you been, son?"

"I miss you, Daddy. When can I see—?"

Kenzie was gone, and an angry female came on the line. "What the hell are you doing?"

"Speaking to my son. Where the fuck are you, bitch?"

"Go fuck yourself, Jason. He's having nothing more to do with you." She hung up.

Sara motioned for Craig to come forward, and she removed the can from her sleeve, sensing that the ex hanging up on him like that could make Jason spiral out of control.

It was a two-pronged attack. Craig jumped Jason from behind. He went down easily, too stunned to retaliate or put up a fight at being caught unaware by the young constable. Sara handed Craig her cuffs, and Will appeared. Between them, they took Jason out of the building. Sara rushed over to untie Nikki from her bindings. Carla entered the warehouse.

"Quick, help me, Carla."

They managed to get Nikki down from the contraption without too much effort and wrapped her in the blanket Carla had sourced from the boot of Sara's car. She was safe, and Jason was in custody.

After instructing Craig and Will to take Jason back to the station, Sara and Carla took Nikki to hospital. On the way, Carla rang Karl Vickers to tell him she was safe and to make arrangements for either him or Shariff to pick Nikki up from the A&E department.

They left Nikki in the capable hands of the nursing staff. She was full of gratitude and relief that she'd come through the ordeal relatively unscathed. They'd take a statement from her later.

Now they were back at the station, Sara found herself getting more and more wound up about the way Jenna Wallace had reacted to Jason speaking with Kenzie and totally understood where the man's frustrations had emerged. *What kind of message did that convey to the child? He sounded so excited to hear his father's voice. Heartbreaking beyond words!*

"Right, now we have the killer sitting in a cell, I want us all to spend the rest of the day tracking down Jenna Wallace."

Carla frowned. "May I ask why?"

Sara looked her in the eye and said, "Because that cow deserves to know the damage she's caused. I want her found and held accountable for this."

"I don't understand. You're going to charge her? With what?"

"No, our hands are tied on that front, but I want her brought in. I'd like to give her a piece of my mind, if nothing else."

Carla shrugged. "Okay."

*F*ive hours later, while Sara was sitting in DCI Price's office bringing the chief up to date with what they'd accomplished, she received a text telling her that Jenna Wallace had been brought into the station. "Sorry, boss, I need to see this woman."

"Go. You have my permission to shit her up a bit. For what it's worth, I think you're doing the right thing. Her type will never learn otherwise."

"Exactly. She's gone too far."

Sara ran down the stairs and into the reception area. The desk sergeant pointed the young woman out, although it was unnecessary for him to do so. Sara immediately recognised the type. She was wearing a black dress that barely covered her backside. There was a slight bump to her middle. Her long brown hair was styled professionally. Hardly the image of a struggling single mum, but then, getting five hundred quid a month for Kenzie, compared to what other single mums received from their exes, was more than a contributing factor to her appearance.

"Miss Wallace, come this way, if you would?" Sara made sure she didn't smile to greet the woman.

She followed Sara up the narrow corridor to the interview rooms.

Once inside, Jenna said, "I don't understand why I'm here."

"Take a seat."

They both sat at the small table.

"I wanted to make you aware of the situation. I didn't have the time to visit you. Thanks for coming in. May I ask where Kenzie is?"

"Why? What concern is it of yours?"

Sara studied every inch of the woman's face and instantly disliked her. "As long as you haven't locked him in a cage alone, I guess I needn't worry."

Jenna's cheeks reddened, and her gaze shifted. "I don't know what you're talking about."

"Is that right? I've done my research on you, young lady. I'm guessing your shenanigans would make a hardened criminal blush. What gives you the right to play god with people's lives? Come on, I'm intrigued to know."

"I don't."

"Really? I find that incredibly hard to believe. Do you have any idea of the damage your evil ways have caused?"

"You're talking in riddles. What do you mean?"

"What I mean is, while you were pulling your ex-partner through the torture rack, using his son as a tool to get back at him for his misgivings, you virtually drove that man to his limits. Women like you should be hung, drawn and quartered in my book."

"How dare you speak to me like that? I demand to speak to your superior. I don't have to take this shit from you or anyone else for that matter."

"I'd willingly bring my superior into this meeting. I'm warning you, though, she'd come down heavier on you than I'm likely to."

"Whatever. I still don't know what you're getting at."

"Let me fill you in then…" And she did. She laid the whole investigation out on the table for Jenna to take in.

The young woman listened without interruption, her expression twisted with different emotions, shock being the dominant one.

"Well, what do you have to say for yourself?"

"Nothing. I can't be held responsible for his actions."

"Can't you? You drove that man to the cliff edge when all he ever wanted to do was spend time with his son. Do you realise how many women out there would love to be in your shoes? Who struggle to make ends meet because the bastards who fathered their children have done a runner and never once put their hands in their pockets? From what I can tell, Jason has never once neglected his duties in that respect, has he?"

Jenna's head dipped. She picked at the skin around her beautifully manicured red talons.

"I can't believe you have nothing to say to that," Sara prompted her. "Why punish him after all he's done for you?"

"You shouldn't listen to everything he tells you."

"Oh, why's that? You don't look like you're a struggling single mother."

"Just because I prefer to dress presentably, it doesn't cover up the fact that he—"

"He what? Loves his son? Wants only what's best for his son? You've not only broken him financially, but mentally, too. You must be so pleased with yourself."

Her mouth clamped shut. Still she refused to look Sara in the eye.

"For your sake, I hope that child never finds out how manipulative and cunning you are."

Her head snapped up at that. "I disagree with you. I've always put Kenzie first."

"I did a little extra digging on you. I have a Cafcass report on you that states differently. Drug and alcohol abuse plus mental abuse of your son. Lady, if you don't buck your ideas up, take it from me, I won't hold back in coming after you."

"Is that some kind of threat?"

"No, it's a bloody promise. You know what?" Sara rose from her chair. "This is one case when I think a child might be better off in care, and believe me, those words have never, ever, left my lips before. This interview is terminated. Get the hell out of my station."

Jenna's uncompromising exterior crumbled in an instant. She knocked her chair over in her haste to leave the room. Her sobs filled the corridor as Sara marched after her.

*Put that in your pipe and smoke it, bitch. I've got you on my radar, you can be sure of that and I'll be passing on my notes to the social to reopen their investigation. I'll throw in Wayne Loddon's statement for good measure as well.*

Sara's next job was one of the most dreadful she'd ever conducted in her career—interviewing Jason Campbell. It took an hour to complete. He laid himself open from the moment Carla hit the record button on the machine. He admitted to all the murders and came across as being full of remorse. Something Sara, in the whole of her police career, had never witnessed before.

Once the interview had finished and Sara had accompanied Jason to the charge suite, she stopped off in the ladies' and released all the pent-up feelings rocking her to the core. She was an emotional wreck after dealing with Jenna Wallace and then having to listen to the trauma she'd put a decent man through over the past two years.

Carla came looking for her five minutes later. Sara was in the process of wiping the mascara trails from her eyes.

"Are you okay?"

"I will be. I don't think I've ever had a case touch me as much as this one."

"Where your sympathy lies with the killer more than the victims?"

"Not sure that's true. Maybe on a par with the victims. Those women shouldn't have died, there's no doubting that. There again, that bitch shouldn't have made up all those lies about Jason and prevented him from seeing the son he so clearly thinks the absolute world of."

"Two wrongs don't make a right as the saying goes." Carla smiled. "I'm sorry for not seeing your perspective during the investigation. After listening to Jason's confession, I know you were right."

Sara spun around and hugged her. "Life can be so unfair, even when we least expect it to be. Come on, let's wrap the paperwork up, or at least make a start on it, and get the hell out of here. And no, I don't fancy a celebratory drink tonight."

"I wasn't going to ask."

# EPILOGUE

*M*ark was thrilled to see her that evening when she eventually rolled up. He hugged her tightly, and not for the first time, she thought how lucky she was to have such a wonderful man in her life.

"I missed you," she said, searching out his lips. His kiss left her breathless.

"Ditto. So did Misty."

They glanced down at Misty who was winding herself in and around the gap between their legs.

"I'll feed her. What's on the menu this evening?"

"Cottage pie and all the trimmings."

"Sounds delicious."

They spent the rest of the evening catching up as if they had been parted for a couple of weeks rather than around forty-eight hours. Then they put their final wedding plans in place.

Sara couldn't wait for the following month. She'd always wanted to be a June bride. She was delighted to see that Mark's enthusiasm matched her own.

In bed, her mind wandered. She couldn't help wondering if his love would continue to grow for her in the future. She swore she loved him more and more each day. The last thing she wanted was to get into a dire situation, one similar to which Jenna and Jason had found themselves in.

"Hey, you were miles away then. Care to share?" he asked.

"Not really. I was just thinking how happy I am right now."

"This is only the beginning, Sara. I swear to you that every day we're together, until our dying day, that is, I will treasure you and treat you like the goddess you deserve to be treated like."

She laughed. "Steady on there. That's quite a statement to uphold."

He kissed her, his intention abundantly clear. Everything else drifted away, nothing else mattered then. Their happiness and future was something she'd cherish forever.

Dear Reader,

What an absolutely heartbreaking read that was, of which certain elements were true.

But as usual, Sara and her team came to the rescue in her own inimitable way. An intriguing tale nevertheless, I'm sure you'll agree.

If you enjoyed this book be sure to pick up the next book in the DI Sara Ramsey series, where Sara tackles a very perplexing case. Run For Your Life

Thank you for your support as always. If you could find it in your heart to leave a review, I'd be eternally grateful, they're like nectar from the Gods to authors.

Happy reading
M A Comley

# KEEPING IN TOUCH WITH THE AUTHOR

Newsletter
http://smarturl.it/8jtcvv

BookBub
**www.bookbub.com/authors/m-a-comley**

Blog
**http://melcomley.blogspot.com**

Join my special Facebook group to take part in monthly giveaways.

Readers' Group

Printed in Great Britain
by Amazon

51598090R00109